TELL-TALE PUBLISHING'S

8TH ANNUAL HORROR ANTHOLOGY

Tell-Tale Publishing's 8th Annual Horror Anthology

The Corner Lot ©2023, Shawn D. Brink
Eclipsed ©2023, Robert Tucker
Death Stalks Darden Place ©2023, Francesca Quarto
The Killing Choice ©2023, Daren Simon
The Overseer ©2023, Daren Simon
But I Won't Do That ©2023, Ric Wasley
The Nightmare Game ©2023, Janet Post
Deliver Us from Evil ©2023, Elizabeth Alsobrooks

Printed in the United States of America

Shawn D Brink

Rob Tucker

Francesca Quarto

Darren Simon

Ric Wasley

Janet Post

Elizabeth Alsobrooks

TABLE OF CONTENTS

THE KILLING CHOICE

Darren Simon

It was just another house, another family. There was nothing special about the two-story Mid-Century Modern-style home nestled quietly in the middle of the suburban block. There was nothing special about the people who resided inside. He didn't hate them. Truth be told, he didn't give them one moment's thought.

It was just another killing choice, like they all were. Just his and his companions' way of having fun.

He drove slowly along the block in his gray SUV, eyes carefully probing for anything out of the ordinary. He'd traveled the street every day for the last couple of weeks. He knew how many cars should be parked along the street, how many in driveways. He knew what homes had children and teens. Husbands and wives. Dogs and cats. He'd paid attention to how many times a week the police would drive through the block. Answer… none.

He had to be careful. Not that he feared for himself. He didn't give a shit about himself. But his woman and his younger brother. Those were the lives he had to protect, even if they were both so annoying, like right now.

"Oh, man, I love this song." His little brother, sitting beside him in the passenger seat, turned up the volume as loud as it could go. *Highway to Hell* blared through the speakers. His brother pounded the dashboard with both fists. "This is the shit."

From behind, his woman laughed wildly. It reminded him of a chicken's cackle. If she wasn't so fucking hot, he would have bashed in her head long ago. "You know it, baby." She sang her words. "I love the shit out of this song. It gets me going."

"Both of you, shut the fuck up." He turned off the radio, glared at his brother, then at his woman through the rearview mirror. She smiled back and blew him a kiss with her large ruby lips. The late afternoon sunlight, angling through the windows, danced off her long blond hair. Her icy blue eyes glimmered.

"What's your problem, Davey?" His dumb-as-shit brother slunk back in his chair, sulking. He feverishly scratched his patchy, thin black beard.

He grabbed his little brother by his clip-on tie. "I told you, Billy, never call me Davey or I'll rip out what few teeth you have left."

"S... sorry, Dave." Billy straightened his tie and his two-sizes too large white collared shirt, which made his scrawny frame seem even thinner. His eyes became glassy. He blinked rapidly. "I'm just no good."

Dave sighed. His fingers tightened on the steering wheel until his knuckles turned white. He knew better than to be hard on Billy. He reached out and rubbed his little brother's scraggly hair. "Sorry, bro. I didn't mean nothing. I just need a little quiet to think. You're the best. I love you, little bro."

Billy smiled wide, revealing crooked, yellow teeth. "I love you, too, Dave."

Dave nodded. "All right, then, let's go have some fun."

"Shit yeah." His woman drank back a Bud, then belched loudly.

"Sunshine, you're all class." Dave rolled his coal black eyes.

She leaned over his seat and planted a wet kiss on his cheek. "You love it, babe. You know I'm the only thing that revs your motor."

She was right. He wasn't about to say it, but it was the truth. Ever since he snatched her, she'd been the only one for him.

"Dave, which one is it?" Billy lifted his hunting knife to his face and licked the blade.

"That one right there." He pointed his finger just up ahead and to the right. He couldn't help but salivate a little. This might have been the fifth one, but it never got old. His pulse quickened. His entire body tingled.

"Oh, babe, I'm gonna be sick." Sunshine mashed her face against the window. "It's so perfect, it makes me want to puke."

Billy laughed.

Dave wiped beads of sweat from his forehead. Sunshine was right. It was too perfect. Beige with white trim, grass in the front freshly mowed and greener than any other yard on the block. Little flowers lined the brick walkway leading up to one of the two-door entryways. A BMW was parked on one side of the driveway. A Lexus SUV right next to it.

He knew inside Mr. Allen Bremmer and his wife, Donna, likely in their forties, probably the kind with office jobs who coached Little League and attended school functions without missing a one, were getting ready for a Sunday dinner. They'd soon call to their kids, Sara, a teenager… yeah, she was a sweet thing… and a younger boy, Tommy, maybe ten or so, to join them at the table.

He'd watched them… closely… a shadow at their windows. He was good at watching… very good.

One thing was for sure. They were boring as shit. Well, maybe not the girl, but Sunshine would never let him have another.

It had to be them.

The Killing Choice

It just felt right… just like the others.

He parked his SUV a few houses down, then turned to his brother. "Billy, do you have your Bible?"

Billy grabbed it from underneath his seat. He marveled at it for just a moment. It was still basically brand new. He'd never really opened it. Had no idea what it said inside. He wasn't one for reading much, and certainly not some holier-than-thou book to tell you how to live your life. Boring. He just wanted to have fun. Still, the dark blue hard cover with gold embroidered lettering was sure pretty to look at.

"Got it right here, Dave." Billy held it up with one hand. With the other, he lifted his old, tarnished revolver. Blotches of dried blood clung to the barrel. "Got my gun, too, and my knife. I'm ready, big bro."

Dave peered back at Sunshine. "You?"

She already had on her Sunday best, taken from a woman she killed last year. It was a light blue blazer jacket, with a flower pattern across the shoulders. It matched her white flower skirt that flowed down to her ankles, hiding the .45 caliber handgun strapped to one thigh and the two daggers strapped to the other.

Sunshine took a swig from a bottle of whiskey. "Let's go have some fun, baby. I've been itching for our next."

Dave smiled wide. Shit, he loved her.

His eyes shifted to both of them before he adjusted his rearview mirror to get a good look at himself. He didn't much like his face when it was clean cut. It showed off the pockmarks from his acne scars, but what the hell. He had to look the part, right? Frowning at himself, he licked his palm, then used it to slick back his short black hair. He lifted his head a bit, just to see what he would look like without a double chin, but there was no getting away from the fat face staring back at him. Too much beer. Too much fast food. Too much of everything.

He winked at his image. "Let's do this."

He slid out of the SUV, taking a moment to grab his brown blazer, which he threw on over his stained white shirt and yellow tie. He then lifted his own slightly worn Bible and tucked it under his arm. Unlike Billy, he'd actually read some passages… and laughed until his belly hurt. Grabbing his own handgun and the eight-inch, gourmet kitchen knife with the sweet pearl handle he'd taken from kill number one, he motioned for Billy and Sunshine to follow him. He also checked his pockets to make sure he had his cigarettes, lighter… and the silencer for his gun.

Straightening his tie and jacket, he gazed wide-eyed at the front door, a thick wooden set of double doors with flowers etched into the wood.

The Killing Choice

He could feel his pulse quickening, thudding against his chest faster and faster. He licked his lips and wiped a bit of saliva from the side of his mouth. His entire body vibrated. The Bremmer's had no idea what was about to befall them.

He shivered as he thought of that moment… that second when they would realize death had come for them and there was no hope.

Oh, he would drink in that fear and feed on their pleas for mercy. The God of the Bible tucked underneath his arm might damn him to hell someday, but who cared. This made him feel alive like nothing else could. What did he care if it meant an eternity of damnation? Fuck, he didn't believe in any of that shit anyway. Once you were dead, there was nothing left—no heaven, no hell—nothing. So, he was going to have as much fun as possible until his time came.

He humbly climbed the brick steps to the front door with Sunshine and Billy close behind. With a quick glance back at both of them, and lifting his Bible up close to his face, he knocked gently on the front door.

Once. Twice. Three times.

Then he waited, holding his breath, tightening his grip on the Bible.

Billy giggled slightly.

Sunshine whispered in his ear. "Oh, baby, you get me so excited when you lead like this."

Darren Simon

Her hot breath brushed against his skin. His knees shook for just a brief moment.

With the click of the door latch, he quickly regained his composure.

The door slightly peeked open, and Mr. Bremmer, his lips parted in a smile, peered through. "Can I help you?"

Can I help you? Such a quaint thing to say. He studied Bremmer in the half second it took the husband and father of two to utter the words. The idiot was dressed well for his Sunday evening family dinner with light blue, buttoned-down, collared shirt and Navy-blue slacks, topped off with a black leather belt and brown leather shoes. Fucking boring. His hair was cut perfectly and the rim of his gold, wire-rimmed glasses clung nicely to his nose.

"I am sorry for this… intrusion… on this lovely evening, but we were wondering if we might have a moment of your time to share the word of God with you." He placed the Bible against his chest and smiled wide.

Bremmer sighed slightly. The smile on his face dimmed just a bit. "Oh, I appreciate that, but we're just sitting down for dinner. Perhaps another time."

"A family dinner—that's lovely, but surely you can spare a moment for our Lord and Savior on this wonderful Sunday."

The Killing Choice

Bremmer started to close the door. "Like I said, perhaps another time. It's getting late, and the sun will be setting soon. I should get back to my family." This time, his face turned grim. He slid back and swung the door closed.

Dave blocked the door with his foot. "How dare you close the door on the Lord. For that, you must be punished."

"What is this?" Bremmer's eyes widened. "Get away from my door."

"I don't think so." Dave thrust out his fist. His knuckles slammed into Bremmer's nose. He enjoyed the crunch of bone and the burst of Bremmer's blood that spilled over his fingers. Bremmer staggered backward, eyes already watering, his hands clutching his broken nose.

Billy and Sunshine rushed through the door. Dave slowly strode in behind them, gently closing the door, then locking it with a click clack. Dropping the Bible on the floor, he reached for the marble handle of his knife. Licking the blood from his fingers, his whole body tingled as if he'd touched a live wire.

It had begun.

Just like the others.

"Honey, what's going on?" Mrs. Bremmer crossed into the living room. Dave studied her to see if his impression of her might change from the times he watched her. No, she was still the blandest woman he'd ever seen in her pink blouse and blue mommy jeans, black hair done tightly in a bun, and little purple scarf around her neck.

"Don't come in—" Bremmer started to say.

Billy smashed his Bible into Bremmer's face. Blood splattered over the cover and against the white wall behind him. Bremmer collapsed to his knees. His head drooped against his chest, blood dripping from his nose and mouth onto his blue shirt and beige carpet.

Mrs. Bremmer screamed. Sunshine leaped at her from the side, slamming her in the gut with a fist, then wrapping an arm around her throat, squeezing tightly until lady Bremmer started coughing and gasping. She whimpered and thrashed her arms, trying to break free. Sunshine held a dagger to her face, and lady Bremmer stopped.

"Don't you utter a sound, bitch." Sunshine gently dragged the blade across her cheek. "I'll cut the shit out of you."

"Mom… Dad?" The teenage Bremmer girl called from the dining room.

"Kids, get out of the house!" Bremmer, his voice thick and garbled, shouted.

Dave motioned to his brother. "Get them."

His little bro disappeared into the other room. There were screams, the sound of glass shattering. Bremmer rose to his feet, stumbling toward the noise.

Dave shook his head, grabbing Bremmer by the throat and aiming the barrel of his gun at his head. "Don't you fucking dare, man. This is happening, and you better accept it, just like the others, 'cause you're weak and ain't a thing you can do to stop this."

Billy, bleeding from a cut to his cheek, lumbered back into the living room, shoving the teen girl and the boy to the ground.

"Dave, they cut me, the little bastards." He rubbed his bleeding cheek. "Let me cut them, Dave. Just a little."

"Leave them alone," Lady Bremmer cried out. She broke free from Sunshine, or rather Sunshine, laughing hysterically, let her go. She threw herself at her children, embracing them, tucking their heads into her shoulders. "They're just children."

"No, no, no, everyone." Dave blinked his eyes and started to walk in a circle around the living room, waving his handgun around as if it were a baton. "This is just terrible. All this violence. It's so unnecessary."

Bremmer spit blood from his mouth. "Listen, you don't need to hurt my family. You can have whatever you want. Money. Jewelry. Anything. Just take it and get out of here. I won't report it.

Just go. I'm telling you, you don't want to do this. It's the wrong choice. Just take what you want and go."

Dave chuckled. His eyes narrowed. His eyes shifted from Bremmer to the teenage girl with her long brown hair and shorts that showed just enough skin for his liking. "You're saying I can have anything I want?"

He started to saunter toward the girl.

"Oh, fuck no." Sunshine grabbed hold of the teenage girl, ripping her from her mom's arms. In the heartbeat it took Lady Bremmer to cry out *please no*, Sunshine dragged the sharp end of her dagger across the girl's throat.

Blood poured from the wound.

"Momma." The girl fell to her knees, grasping her neck, then onto her side. She coughed and wheezed… then was silent. Her blood spilled around her body.

Lady Bremmer squealed, reaching for her daughter. "No!'

Bremmer threw himself on Billy, but the younger man was too fast. He dug his knife into Bremmer's gut over and over, ten, twelve, fifteen times, until Bremmer crumbled to the floor like a raggedy doll, blood pooling around him.

"Shit Sunshine, what the hell?" Dave crossed to her, then slapped her in the face. He loved her, but she ruined everything. It was supposed to be slow. She was supposed to let him enjoy this. How could she take that away from him?"

Sunshine rubbed her cheeks and smiled viciously. She grabbed him by the collar and pulled him closer. "I didn't like the way you looked at her. I'm your only one." She pressed her lips against his so hard it actually hurt before shoving him away. "Don't you forget that."

"I'm going to kill you all." Lady Bremmer rose to her feet.

Billy leaped on her from behind, forced her to the ground. Placing a pillow from the couch over her head, he blew out her brains point blank. It sounded like little more than a thud. Her body spasmed, then she stopped moving.

"Well, fuck. This wasn't fun at all." Dave lifted a silencer from his pocket and attached it to his handgun. "Sorry, little man." Without hesitating, he shot the Bremmer boy through the heart. The boy didn't make a sound. He fell backward, let out one final breath… and died.

Dave slumped onto the couch. This was all wrong. It was nothing like the others. Nothing at all. Well, at least they could enjoy the family's house for a day or two and slowly watch the Bremmer's rot before heading out in search of the next kill.

"Sunshine, I ought to—"

Darren Simon

"I... told you... you made a... bad... choice." Bremmer gasped out the words. His body, still crumpled like trash on the ground, didn't budge. He stared at Dave with vacant eyes. He sighed one last time, then was quiet. His eyes remained open but empty... and fixed on Dave.

***

He wiped the last bit of pot roast juice from his mouth, then belched. Damn, that lady Bremmer could cook. Sure as hell better than Sunshine. He patted his stomach while reaching for a cigarette from his pant pocket, which he ignited with the golden lighter he'd taken from kill number three. Sitting back, he took a long swig of beer, then gazed through the dining room window. Night had come, casting the neighborhood in darkness.

"Sure was nice of the Bremmers to stock up their fridge." He took one more long drink, then puffed on his cigarette. The smoke circled his face. "Thank you, Bremmer family."

He nodded to the bloody corpses of the Bremmers. He'd sat them up in chairs around the table, their bodies drooping, shoulders sagging. Their heads hung loosely from their necks. He'd made sure to keep Bremmer's eyes open.

The Killing Choice

He lifted his beer to Bremmer. "Sorry, friend, it was all in good fun. I hope you'll understand. In a way, you're lucky. I didn't get to make you suffer like the others."

Bremmer's body caved in. His head slumped until it struck the table with a crack.

"Fuck me." Dave's body tensed. A breath lodged in his throat. "Shit, Sunshine, you see that? Think Bremmer here is pissed at me?"

Sunshine licked her plate, then threw it against the wall. It splintered into pieces that sprayed around the dining room. "I'm still angry at you, babe."

"What for, love bug?"

"You wanted that scrawny little teen bitch."

He laughed. She wasn't really wrong, but he knew better. He never would have touched her. Killed her, yes. That was part of the game. But touched her, no. "Sunshine, how many times do I have to tell—"

"Dave, you got to see this." That was Billy calling from some other part of the house.

"Dang, Billy, can't it wait?" He shouted. "I'm having dinner with the Bremmers."

"You need to see this," Billy answered.

Dave noted concern in his brother's voice. "Where you at, little bro."

"The basement."

He sighed. Rising from the table, he bowed to the Bremmer corpses. "Excuse me, Bremmers." Then, he turned to his woman. "Sunshine, get your sweet ass up and walk with me. Time for you to forgive me. I've forgiven you for spoiling my fun."

She didn't utter a word. Grabbing her knife, she followed him through the house to a hallway just past the kitchen. There, they found the door that led to the basement. Billy had switched on the light, but its dim luminance did little to light the way, shedding more shadows than anything else. Dave was the first to step through the door; Sunshine followed close behind.

"Let's go take a shower, baby," she whispered into his ear. "I got that teen's blood all over me. It makes me sick."

"You know, you go do that," he said. "I love you, sugar thing, but you kind of smell sour."

She smacked the back of his head. "Fuck you, I might not let you have me tonight." With that, she disappeared through the door.

He continued on his way until he reached the bottom of the stairs. His eyes raced over the room. It was like another family room with a couch, a couple of rocking chairs and a big-screen TV mounted on the wall. Recessed lighting in the ceiling cast the room in a soft white glow, but some of the lights were out, which left a shadowy haze on the walls.

Billy was across the room. He turned when he saw his older brother. "Dave, check this shit out. It's like a fucking cave or something."

"What are you talking about?" He crossed to Billy, who stood beside what looked like a steel door, several inches thick. He peered through. Billy was right. Inside was what he could only describe as a cavern. Probably manmade. There was no way to tell how far back it extended. Darkness hid the tunnel's end. Unlit torches lined either side of the walls. *What twisted fuck were the Bremmers up to?*

Billy pointed to the cavern's wall. "And what do you make of this?"

He followed his little bro's finger. It pointed to scratch marks all over the walls. He peered closer. The scratch marks extended as far as he could see. "What the—"

From behind them, the lights in the basement flickered.

Somewhere in the house, Sunshine suddenly screamed.

The blood rushed from Dave's head. A chill spread through his limbs. His pulse raced but not from excitement this time. This was not a sensation he was used to. He stared at Billy. His little brother's skin turned white.

Darren Simon

This was not like the others… definitely not.

The lights still flickered. From somewhere came the sound of sizzling as if bacon were cooking on the stove. Something nearby breathed heavy.

Sunshine screamed again, louder than the first.

He tightened his grip on his gun, then ran through the basement, aware Billy was right behind him.

His mind swirled. Nothing made Sunshine scream. She made others scream. She was the fiercest woman's he'd ever met. That's why he couldn't kill her. That's why he had to make her his own. So, for her to be scared of anything… what the hell?

With Billy right behind him, he charged up the stairs, following the sound of her screams, and there was something else.

A vicious growl echoed around them.

The Bremmers had a dog? In all the time he'd watched them, he'd never seen a single pet. Had they hidden the beast in that cave?

Once up the stairs, he bolted along a hallway lined with family photos, turned the corner into the master bedroom… and slid to a stop. His mouth dropped open. Eyes widened. Heart, for just a second stopped beating.

The Killing Choice

Under the white glow of a lamp, the biggest dog he'd ever seen had Sunshine cornered. Only it wasn't like any other dog. This beast stood upright on its hind legs with bulging, pulsating muscles rippling under black fur.

"What the fuck is that?" Billy stuttered his words.

The beast peered back at them with bright yellow eyes bulging from its head. Its massive snout opened wide, bearing dagger length teeth. Drool slid from between its quivering lips. Dave's eyes focused on something else—a purple scarf around the thing's neck.

"Help me," Sunshine begged. She was backed against the wall. Her naked body already cut up, blood seeping down her chest to her legs. Torn skin hung from slash marks across her face. "Baby, I don't want to die."

Dave froze.

Billy didn't. He opened fire on the beast. Several rounds struck its back. It reared back and roared.

Billy's hands shook, but he fired again. "Fuck—"

Something from behind grabbed Billy and dragged him away. He continued to fire, rounds ricocheting off the walls, until his gun was silenced.

Darren Simon

Dave, his body stiff as a statue, shifted his eyes back to Sunshine.

The beast howled one more time, then drove its razor-sharp claws into her gut. Sunshine shrieked. Her pupils slid up into her head. The beast ripped out her insides, her blood splashing all over Dave. He still didn't move, even as warm bits of her entrails dripped down his cheek. The beast held up Sunshine's organs like some trophy, then bit into them like a wild dog.

Blood spewed from Sunshine's mouth. Somehow still alive, she looked at him and whimpered. With one hand, she reached for him.

He didn't reach back.

The beast opened its mouth as wide as possible, and sank its fangs into her face, tearing out her eyes, nose, her flesh.

Nothing remained but her bloody skull and her long blond hair.

The beast threw what was left of her body against the far wall. She landed with a smack, more of her entrails bloodying the walls, like some freakshow art exhibit, then she crumbled to the floor.

Dave shook his head and finally unfroze. Stumbling backward, he quickly scrambled on his hands and knees out of the room. Gazing back just once, he saw the yellow eyes of the beast watching him, its head turned to one side as if studying its next prey. *Oh. God. Please, don't let it get me.* Somehow, he climbed to his feet and ran down the stairs.

He had to get Billy and get...

His little brother lay in pieces on the living room floor. Two smaller... dogs... savaged his body, chewing threw his insides. Their snouts were covered in his blood. His flesh coated their fangs. *Billy, no. I'm so sorry.* His brother's head, eyes torn out, lay on one side of the room. His arms on another. His legs on top of the couch.

"Billy!" Dave, rage burning his insides, raised his gun to fire on the two creatures. "Fucking die, dogs."

A clawed hand grabbed the gun and ripped it from his fingers. "You've done enough damage, friend," a heavy, throaty voice uttered.

Dave turned and wet his pants. Standing before him was Bremmer. His eyes glowed bright yellow. His skin sizzled and popped. The bones in his cheeks expanded, cutting through his flesh. His cleanly shaven face was sprouting hair. He breathed heavily, painfully. He raised his lips in a smile, revealing fangs ripping through his teeth.

The beast with the purple scarf slowly climbed down the stairs on all fours and slid behind Bremmer. The two smaller dogs maneuvered beside him. All three growled at Dave, their yellow unblinking eyes locked on him.

Darren Simon

Bremmer took a step closer to him. "I told you this was a mistake." His voice was different. Deep. Scratchy. Garbled. Each word followed by a heavy breath. "But you didn't listen."

Dave forced himself to speak. "What are you?"

Bremmer laughed. His skin popped louder. His head tilted from one side to the other. His back cracked and arched unnaturally, causing him to hunch over. His face pulsated. He grimaced, then slowly stood straight. "Look out the window, friend. Tell me what you see."

"Please, I don't want to die like this." Dave could barely stand. His limbs trembled. The gun slid from his shaking fingers.

"I said tell me what you see." Bremmer growled out the words.

Dave peered over Bremmer's shoulder at the living room window. Through the spaces between the blinds, he saw the moon.

It was full. Bright. Yellow. Looming large over the night.

"Do you see it?" Bremmer breathed in deeply. His arms and legs cracked and twisted into unnatural positions. His jaw dislodged. The skin on his face shredded and fell away. He reared his head back as his mouth split wide open, and a wolf's snout thrust through.

The Killing Choice

Dave shut his eyes. Maybe if he closed them, this would all just disappear. Sunshine would still be alive. His brother, too. This would be just another kill. Like all the others. "Yes," he mumbled through shivering lips. "I see."

"Then you know what we are." Bremmer dropped to all fours. His clothes tore away from his body, leaving him naked. Brown fur tore through his skin.

"Yes." Dave kept his eyes closed. Tears slid through his sealed eyelids. Spittle dropped from his mouth.

Bremmer inched closer to him. "It's all true, friend. Werewolves. Creatures of the dark. We exist. And you should know from the tales, the only way to kill our kind is with silver."

Dave fell to his knees. He ripped at his hair. "Please."

Bremmer's face was almost fully wolf now. His words came slow and rough. "My wife and I... we've learned to control our hunger. Our cubs, though, are still learning. That's why we have the cave below. To keep them and your world safe. They're good wolves, yet you would seek to deprive them of their lives for your own sick entertainment."

"I'm so sorry." Dave tucked his head into his chest.

"Don't be." Bremmer laughed again. It was guttural and harsh. "We'll feed on you for days. Thank you, friend."

Dave had one final thought before the end came.

This was not like the others at all.

ECLIPSED

Rob Tucker

She feared opening the front door and going outside the house. She stopped taking care of herself. Her lack of hygiene and the odor of her unwashed body reminded her of decay and brought her closer to her child. She prepared and ate only her son's favorite foods, chicken nuggets, PBJs (peanut butter and jelly sandwiches), veggie burgers, and pizza.

After the first time listening to the counselor's explanation about dealing with the loss of a child, she refused to continue with grief counseling. She didn't want to heal. She didn't want to move on. She wanted to bring her son back.

Betty Smith thought her discovery was a projection of her grief over the death of her son. While the memories of his young life were still fresh, she spent much of her time gazing at his photos celebrating his achievements and revisiting the toys that had been instrumental to his learning through play and imagination.

His oft-stated plan was to play all day.

He had collected nearly one hundred small cars and trucks that he assiduously organized and maintained according to their roles, particularly the fire trucks, police cars, ambulances, dump trucks, and heavy construction equipment trucks.

She filled the bath with warm water and imagined him chattering to his boats and toys floating about in the tub. She read his children's stories to him as though he were cuddling next to her at bedtime even though he was physically not there. She talked to him about the characters drawn in the books and the meaningful lessons they conveyed. She tucked the blankets under his chin and kissed his forehead as though he lay on his pillow clutching his favorite animal, a brown and white stuffed dog.

She castigated herself for ever telling him he had an attitude when he was hangry (hungry and angry) and sassed her and retorted, "You have attitude. You're a bad mother. I'm not going to play with you anymore."

He selected the clothes he liked to wear and dressed himself. He especially liked bright colored shirts.

He had carefully observed their behaviors and repeated what they said as his language increased and the comprehension of his world grew.

At first, she hadn't understood his fascination with body parts and his preoccupation with farts and burps and bodily functions. "I'm farting on you."

"That's for the bathroom," she had said. "We don't talk about farting at the dinner table. When you burp, you say excuse me."

He burped and giggled hilariously. He found his parents and life amusing and vastly entertaining.

He wanted to help do everything they did, including mixing cookie dough and pancake batter while standing on his stepstool at the kitchen counter.

He had learned how to use simple hand tools by helping his dad with house repairs.

One day, he had slouched into the kitchen while she was washing dishes. He expelled a great sigh.

"What is it, Sweetness," she asked upon seeing his despondent expression.

He shrugged his thin shoulders. "I don't have the time to do all the things I want to do."

She stooped and scooped him into her arms. "Oh, I know how you feel, Dear. I know only so well. Your Daddy and I feel the same way."

Her husband silently watched from the doorway.

Video games had been among the boy's most recent playtime influences. Although she had observed him playing the games, she had never tried them herself until now.

She hoped for some reconnection to her little boy by keeping the artifacts and events of his life in the forefront of her thoughts, never allowing them to fade or be replaced by her mundane day to day activities. Spiritually interacting with the artifacts of her child was a ritual that did not lessen the pain of loss and the rage at the cause of her son's murder.

The reporting of mass murders by deranged psychotics with assault weapons had become standard in the news media. Betty's belief that the killings would not touch their lives had been shattered. All school-age children were vulnerable. There was no escape from the possibility that any child could become a victim.

She wanted to strike back against the political and economic influences that placed innocent targets in the crosshairs of demented gun owners and their distortion of the Second Amendment. She wanted vengeance where none was available.

She could not erase the event and scene from her mind of the flashing red and blue lights and wailing sirens of emergency vehicles and of shouted directions over a bullhorn and an army of heavily armed police officers marching a line of children to an area where screaming hysterical parents waited to claim them.

Paramedics were removing small corpses concealed in black body bags from the school building to a convoy of ambulances crowding the adjoining streets and parking lot.

Her mind swam in a morass of streaming images on the video screen. Only one image was placid and clear. Her child had been intrigued by stories of space travel through the galaxies. His interest had brought her again and again to the animated sequence of planets orbiting around the sun. The software gave the viewer the remote option of manually manipulating the positions of the planets. She remembered her son's enjoyment at recreating the planetary locations like colored marbles in outer space. She wasn't a religious person, but she wanted to believe that he existed somewhere out there.

Something happened outside her house windows when she positioned the moon between the earth and the sun. The neighborhood grew dark. After a few minutes, she shifted the moon to another location and restored the sunlight.

Again, she tried positioning the moon between the sun with the same effect. An electric impulse of excitement surged through her body. She leaped up from her chair and charged out of the house. Darkness blanketed the city.

Rob Tucker

She reentered the house and sat at the computer. She moved the moon and daylight returned.

When her husband, Jerry, returned from work, he found Betty at the computer viewing the unscheduled solar eclipse and watching the newscast of global disasters.

"Jerry, come and look at this," she shouted. "Look what I found. Look what I can do. Kip is talking to us."

He did not dispute her claim that she had made contact with their son. He believed she had lost her mind from grief.

He suppressed his own despair over the loss of their son and the mental decline of his wife. He missed her sunny expression and uplifting laughter, her teasing harassment, and the many hugs they shared with their boy. With their son's death, she seemed to have vacated their life together or their life had vacated them.

He would never forget their son's excitement at the discovery of his first "wobbly tooth," learning to ride his bicycle without training wheels, visits to the playground jungle gyms, touch tag racing around with other children shouting in high spirits, the importance of making and having friends.

His gangly long legs and growing feet had shoved and pushed him out of bed when Kip, upset by a nightmare, came from his room and crawled into bed with them.

He remembered the potty training not so long ago when their little boy's voice rang out from the bathroom, "I pooped! Dad, will you come and wipe my butt!"

The eclipse did not go away. It did not end. The planetary orbit remained at a standstill.

Media newscasts, religious leaders and viewers exhorted that humanity was being punished and that the end of the world was happening.

Betty knew what was happening. It was not the mythological belief of a vengeful God. She knew she controlled what was happening right there on her son's video game computer.

After just one month, environmental and social impacts changed their lives. Crumbling roads and collapsing bridges stalled transportation. Thousands of acres of dead and dying crops on once fertile farmlands curtailed food production. Corporations failed and banks closed. Grocery store shelves emptied with the ensuing competition for food and water. Rising tides eroded shorelines and flooded coastal towns and cities.

One day, Jerry answered a loud knock at the front door and confronted two men wearing black suits.

Rob Tucker

"Yes, can I help you?"

"We're from the Federal Government. We need to talk to you and your wife."

"What do you want? We haven't done anything."

"Don't let them in," Betty shouted from behind him. "Don't let them in."

"We have traced the source of the solar eclipse. We are seizing your computer."

"That's ridiculous. We don't have anything to do with the eclipse. If anything, it's being caused by global warming."

"Global warming doesn't cause an eclipse. Just let us in. Stay out of the way. We'll take the computer and be gone."

Betty screamed. "No, no, the computer belongs to our son. That's how he communicates with us."

"Your son is dead, Mrs. Smith. He doesn't communicate with anybody."

"Go away! Leave us alone!"

"Your wife is delusional," said the taller of the men in black. "Get control of her or we will. Now, move aside and let us in."

"Hold on. Hold on. You can't come in without a warrant."

"In matters like this, we don't need a warrant."

"I'm sorry. I don't believe you."

The bulked-up partner dislodged Jerry with a strong flat-handed shove to the chest that sent him wheeling back off-balance. Both intruders charged into the living room. With a raging snarl, Betty leaped in front of them. They grabbed her and forced her to the floor. She screamed in pain as her twisted arm reached the breaking point.

Jerry pulled at the shoulder of the taller man and tried to punch him. "Don't touch her. Get your hands off her."

"If you resist, you will both be handcuffed and placed under arrest."

"Who the hell are you anyway? You don't have the right to force your way in here. You aren't Federal agents."

"We have every right. Now, you and your wife cooperate or you're going to get hurt." He pulled out a handgun from under his coat.

"For God's sake, don't shoot us."

"Then just stay quiet and out of the way. Don't try to stop us. Get the computer," he said to his partner.

They knew exactly in what room the computer was located. Minutes later, they were gone.

Betty sobbed, "They aren't who they say they are."

"How do you know? How can you tell?"

"They have our son," said Betty. "They have stolen our son."

"No, they haven't. Stop that. Who are they?"

"They're predators. I know they're predators. They're harvesting dead children through video games."

"That's impossible. How do you know?"

"Don't question me. I just know."

"But Kip was murdered in a mass shooting."

"Exactly my point. The gun crazies are all a part of it. They're all a part of the conspiracy to destroy our children."

"Betty, that's just in your head. There is no conspiracy."

"There is. There is. We have to stop them. We have to stop them."

"Kip is gone. We must accept that."

"They've abducted his spirit."

Jerry shook his head. "This is beyond us. We can't bring him back."

Betty's face contorted in a way that terrified him. "We have to try. We have to find a way."

One week later, the solar eclipse moved on and daylight returned to its normal cycle.

Then, a mass killing occurred at an elementary school two-thousand miles away.

THE OVERSEER

Darren Simon

I stared through the blinds, eyes wide, mouth open even wider, at the cemetery visible from what was to be my bedroom window. It wasn't right beneath. There was a brick wall and a dirt service road in between.

Still, from my window, I had a clear view of aging tombstones and decaying statues with gray eyeless faces turned toward the heavens or some shit, worn by time and this damned desert heat. I shook my head, closed the blinds, then turned to my mom. "What the hell, Mom, you want us to live next to a cemetery?"

The sun blazed against the window. Temps outside sweltered at 110 degrees. Somewhere in the house, the air conditioner moaned as it wheezed out a trickling of cool air that stunk of burnt car oil.

The best it could do was cast the house in a warm, thick 80 degrees, but it was livable. Better than outside where the heat made my sweat simmer against my skin and my T-shirt and jeans feel like hot, wet rags clinging to my body.

I was literally sweating my balls off outside.

Inside, the warmth just felt heavy, like a weight bearing down on my shoulders.

My mom offered a slight smile. "I know, baby, but this is only temporary. We're just renting this place until I can find a house for us to buy."

Mr. Hanson, the owner, placed his large, meaty hand on my shoulder. "What are you afraid of, kid, a few ghosts, maybe a zombie or two? Afraid they'll come for you in the night? Drag you off to hell?"

He unleashed a bellowing, mucous-filled, throaty laugh. The stench of cigarettes and hard liquor leaked through his hot breath. I nudged his hand away, then turned to face him. He towered over me with a muscular frame covered by a sweat-stained Hawaiian shirt unbuttoned enough to show graying chest hair and tight beige khakis that showed off his junk way too much. His lips curled back revealing yellow teeth. His coal black eyes were set deep within his leathery face. I was pretty sure his jet-black hair was fake.

None of that made me hate him.

It was the way he looked at my mom.

His eyes shifted from me to her. "Now, little girl," he said to her in an unsettling voice, "if there is anything you need, you feel free to reach out to me any time day… or night, and I'll make sure to get right over here to fulfill your needs." He wiped beads of sweat from his forehead and took a step toward her.

My mom smiled but backed away. "Thank you, but I'm sure we'll be fine."

Mr. Hanson moved closer to her. "It's just that I know it can get lonely with you being new in town and not having a man to care for you."

I balled my hands into fists. My knuckles turned white. My heart thudded louder and louder. My mom shook her head at me.

Her smile disappeared. Mr. Hanson was a fool. He didn't know my mom well. She wasn't one to take shit from anyone. Her normally kind face turned to stone. Her icy blues eyes narrowed.

"Like I said, Mr. Hanson, we'll be fine." Her voice was sharp, like a razor's edge. She crossed to the door and pushed it open, a clear sign for him to leave my bedroom and the house. "Now, sir, if you wouldn't mind, my son and I have some unpacking to do."

Mr. Hanson blinked, then bowed to my mom. He started toward the door but stopped before leaving. He sneered at her and leaned in a bit closer. "You have a nice day, and remember, there are ways to lower the re—"

"Don't you think you should be getting home to Mrs. Hanson, Mr. Hanson." My mom crossed her arms. She didn't bother to look at him.

DARREN SIMON

He nodded before gazing once more at me with a nod. Coughing up a bit of phlegm, then swallowing it again, he lumbered from the room, down the stairs and out the front door.

"Mom, we can't stay here." I crossed to her. "That guy's a sleaze. If he tries to touch you, I swear I'll kill him. I will. I'll kill him if I get the chance. If dad were here, he'd—"

"I know, Jimmy." Mom reached out and wrapped me in a hug. My face was buried in her long blond hair. Even in this dusty, rotten place, her hair smelled of sweet flowers. "But it's just the two of us, and I promise I can take care of us. And your father is always watching over us, keeping us safe."

I pushed away. "Mom, why here?"

She tilted her head. Her eyes softened. "Because the school district needed a psychologist, and I needed a job to support us."

"This place sucks." I turned away from her and focused on my room's plain pale blue walls, each one covered by brown scuff marks (I hoped it wasn't dried crap) with far too many nails hammered into the plaster. "We can do better than this."

My mom placed her arm around my shoulders. "And we will."

THE OVERSEER

I peeked out the window again at the cemetery and the tombstones visible amid a sea of dry yellowing grass.

"Mom, not by a cemetery… really."

"I didn't know, Jimmy, but you're fifteen." She lowered her head and took a deep breath. "I know it's asking a lot, but I need you to be okay with this, just for a little while. If you give me a chance, I'll get us into a nice house far away from here, and you might even find this change will be good for us. Now, let's finish unloading the car."

I sighed. "Okay."

Once more, my eyes swept across the cemetery.

A man with long hair in dark overalls appeared. He stood rigidly next to a tombstone. He held the handle to a shovel in one hand. My body froze for some reason. My breath lodged in my throat. His head, covered by a baseball cap, was bowed, but for an instant he gazed up—and at me. A shadow masked his face, but I could see his wide, unnatural grin and his eyes. They glowed yellow.

I turned to my mom. "Mom, look at this guy in the cemetery. He's freaking me out."

My mom stepped to the window. "What guy? Jimmy, don't let your imagination get the best of you."

DARREN SIMON

I peered back at the cemetery. He was gone as if he'd never been there. Maybe he hadn't.

My limbs still trembled.

***

I lay shirtless in my bed, my jeans unbuttoned but still glued to my legs. My bed sheets, damp from sweat, were a welcome relief from the Valley's summer night. The whine of the air conditioner was a constant reminder that even well past midnight not even the darkness could drive away the musty desert heat.

Sleep was impossible. Blinking hard, I pondered the cobwebs hanging from the ceiling of my darkened room, lit only by beams of moonlight slicing through my blinds.

"This sucks." I ran my fingers through my wet brown hair, mainly just to unstick strands of it from my forehead. With my other hand, I tried to rub away the salty burning sensation searing my eyes.

Turning onto my side, I focused on the framed photograph of Dad sitting on my bedside table. I remember him smiling even when times were tough. He was always ready with a joke when I needed to hear one. He could lift my spirits with just a wink. But, in this photo, he looked so serious in his police uniform. *Damn you for leaving us, for leaving me. Why couldn't you have been more careful. Now, here mom and I are trapped in this armpit of a town.*

"Fuck this, I need to get out of this shithole." I jumped out of bed, threw a white T-shirt over my thin frame and paced my room, the wooden floor creaking under my feet. "Where you going to go, fool? You can't abandon Mom."

I dropped back onto my bed, head lowered to my chest.

Unseen fingers suddenly brushed against my cheek.

I peered up, expecting to see that mom had walked into my room, but I was alone. Maybe it had just been an extra puff from the air condi—

"Jimmy." A voice as whispery as the wind called to me.

I climbed to my feet, pulse spiking, a hollow feeling in my gut making it hard to breathe. "Uh, Mom?"

"Jimmy, see me." The voice was distant, mumbled.

"What the hell? Mom, is this a prank?"

There was no response.

I clutched at my throat, forcing myself to take a breath.

The voice went quiet.

Great, now I was hearing things. I chuckled softly and unclenched every muscle in my body.

DARREN SIMON

One day, and this place is already driving me crazy.

I focused on the blinds. "Wonder what that stupid cemetery looks like at night."

I inched toward the window. For some crazy reason, every step was harder than the one before as if trying to lift my feet out of mud. My chest ached and my hands felt clammy. *What are you afraid of, wimp?* I licked dry lips. *Nothing, especially some voice in my head.*

Once at the window, I paused. I didn't need to look through the blinds. I could just turn around, go downstairs, and grab a Coke from the fridge, then stay awake until daylight and convince Mom that we have to get out of here.

Ignoring my own advice and the pain intensifying in my gut, I lifted a shaky hand to the blinds, then slightly cracked them open. Slowly, I edged my face closer to the glass. The little hairs on the back of my neck stood at attention. My stomach was queasy. An icy tremor shot down my back.

"Please don't be there," I whispered. "Don't be—"

Under the spotlight of a glimmering full moon, the stranger in dark overalls stood next to the same tombstone, lips parted in an eerie grin. A whimper slipped from my mouth. Shallow breaths raced from my throat. His yellow eyes gazed at my house. As if at that moment he saw me peek through the window, his head slightly tilted to the side. In his hands was no shovel. It was an axe.

My body twitched. I let go of the blinds. Stumbled backward, falling onto the floor. I sat there, lacing my fingers until my knuckles turned white.

"Jimmy, see me." The voice, guttural and deep, crept through my mind.

I squeezed my eyelids closed and covered my ears. Still on my ass, I rocked back and forth, grinding my teeth. *Get out of my head.* This couldn't be real. It was just a stupid nightmare. *Wake the fuck up.*

The voice went quiet. The only sound was the deafening beat of my heart, throbbing in my ears, pounding heavily against my skull.

I slowly opened my eyes and crawled back to my window.

"Don't be there." I stuttered the words through a clenched jaw. "God, don't let him be there."

Blinking away sweat and tears, I lifted the blinds again… and my body sagged. Shoulders relaxed. He wasn't.

I collapsed to the floor. *You see, it's just—*

"Jimmy, see me." The lamp on my desk flickered on and off. *No!* The blinds slid up on their own. I stood on trembling legs and glanced at the window. Yellow eyes glared back at me from right

outside. Blood rushed from my head. *No, God!* The locks on the window unlatched. I backed into the wall behind me and tried to mash myself through the plaster. My eyes bulged from their sockets. I started to hyperventilate.

"Mom, help me! Mom!"

"Jimmy, your time has come."

Fingers, more bone than flesh, slowly pried open the window. I tried to look away, but unseen hands gripped my head, painfully twisting it to face the window. More invisible fingers pried my eyes open. I thrashed my arms and legs but couldn't break the grip.

With jerky movements, bones cracking in deadly rhythm, the *thing* climbed through my window.

First, one massive leg in torn, muddied overalls and a thick black boot crossed over, followed by an arm covered in decaying flesh.

"Mom!" I screamed. "Mom, please, Mom!"

"She won't hear you, Jimmy. No one will hear your screams." The *thing's* head was next to cross through. Rotting, bloody flesh hung like a mask over an exposed skull. Scraggly long, dark hair stuck out from underneath a baseball cap. Each breath it took was a labored, wet hiss. *This isn't happening! Jesus, let me wake up!* The *thing's* yellow eyes bulged as if they would pop out of its head. Black goo dripped from the sides

of its mouth. The clicking of its bones wouldn't stop. It drove me mad.

"Please, God!" I pleaded. "Don't let this... thing... kill me."

"No God can help you, Jimmy, for you have been chosen." The beast was now fully in my room, standing before me. In its skeletal hands was a two-sided battle axe, the steel cracked, the sides covered in blotches of something dark.

"Who are you?" My words came as barely a whisper. "How do you know my name?"

"I am the Overseer." He crossed to me, his head tilted to one side, mouth twisted in a mangled smile. He stopped in front of me. More ooze dripped from his lips. A hot, green mist drifted from his mouth with each phlegmy breath. The stench of rotting eggs made my eyes water. The beast inched its decomposing face even closer and brushed a finger against my cheek.

The Overseer? I begged my body to break free and run, but I just couldn't.

"You should rejoice, Jimmy, for the spirits have chosen you to take my place. You are to become the Overseer." The beast kissed me on the forehead with lips as dry as sandpaper. A thick, dark mucus dripped from my brow onto my cheeks. *"Take heart, boy. You are to be reborn in the service of the dead this night."*

"What are you talking about? Please, just let me go."

"*I cannot.*" He lifted his head away and slowly, deliberately licked his axe. His smile widened. "*I understand you do not wish this gift that has been bestowed upon you, so I will offer another, and then you will have no choice but to accept your destiny. Take my hand and come with me.*"

"No, just leave me—"

The Overseer grabbed me by the neck, then lifted me into the air. He slammed me into the wall next to my door. I heard the crunch of plaster splintering behind me. Blinding pain shot through my head. His smile disappeared. I grabbed at his hand, but it was like a vise slowly crushing my throat, cutting off my air. My chest burned. "*If you do not do as I say, I will have no choice but to take your mother in your place. Is that what you want, Jimmy?*"

No, not my mom. I dropped my hands and stopped fighting. He lowered me to the floor and released his grip. My legs wobbled, and I fell to my hands and knees. Pain radiated from my back and head. Rubbing my throat, I thirstily drank in as much air as I could. "No, I'll do as you say."

The Overseer's smile returned. "*I know you will. What choice is there?*"

THE OVERSEER

A sorrowful gray fog swept into my room through the open window, snaking across the floor, creeping toward me. My eyes widened. Mouth hung wide. That was no fog. Ghostly beings, men and women, even little children, crawled along the floor, their empty eyes locked on me, their hands reaching for me.

Their moans seeped into my ears.

The Overseer beckoned them on with a wave of his hand. *"You see, Jimmy, they are so excited to welcome you."*

He gazed at them like an adoring parent, then turned back at me with his twisted smile. *"Greet them, Jimmy, for you will care for them with all the love that I have shown them."*

"Stop saying my name." I turned toward my door, but something spun me around to face the dead. "Don't let them take me. I said I'd go with you. Isn't that enough? I'm begging you."

"Do not fear, boy." The Overseer let loose a bellowing laugh.

The crawling wraiths reached my feet, then slunk up my leg, their touch like a freezing snowstorm that burns the skin. The black holes in place of their eyes joined into an abyss about to swallow me whole. Their arms and legs wrapped around my stomach, my chest and my neck, squeezing my insides until they might explode. I tried to scream, but the searing chill of their embrace iced my breath away.

I yelped, then the world around me slipped into a gray vacuum, except for the Overseer's yellow eyes, which blazed through the darkness. The last thing I heard was his shrieking laugh and the moans of the dead.

And my own silent scream.

***

"Open your eyes and behold my gift to you."

The Overseer's words were muted as if spoken from far away. My head spun, and I had to fight to keep down vomit. Shaking off dizziness, I fought the growing madness deep inside that made me want to tear my hair out. I was awake enough to know my eyes were shut, but I didn't want to open them. If I kept my eyes closed, maybe I could pretend this wasn't happening. Once I opened them… there was no hope.

My head felt heavy and hung against my chest. My nostrils burned from the putrid stench of God knows what. I shivered despite the heated air filling my lungs. Still, I kept my eyes closed and didn't dare utter a sound.

Hands grabbed my hair and wrenched my head up. I grimaced, but my eyes remained sealed.

THE OVERSEER

"I said, open your eyes, boy."

Someone else groaned. *Oh my God, Mom! Did he take my mom?*

My eyes fluttered open. Hands clamped into fists. "If you hurt—"

In that instant, as the blurriness slid away, I saw who whimpered, Mr. Hanson, the sleazy owner of our rental.

He lay on top of a gray, cracked sarcophagus, still dressed in his Hawaiian shirt and tight khakis. Blood dripped from his mouth, slid down his neck and created a thick, red pool on the ground. His arms and legs were spread apart and chained. His eyes bulged. The only sound he made was a gurgling whimper, and he wouldn't stop.

His eyes found me, and he tried to scream, but it came out as a terrified squeal. More blood sprayed from his mouth.

The Overseer stood over him, axe in one hand, something I couldn't quite make out in his other.

"Care to feast on this man's tongue? The beast held out his hand to me. *"I so prefer fresh meat."* Without waiting for my response, he lifted his hand to his mouth, and bit down on what I now knew was Mr. Hanson's tongue, gnawing at it as if chewing a piece of gum. Black goo slid from his own mouth.

DARREN SIMON

My stomach roiled. On my knees, I dry-heaved. When it was over, gasping for air, my eyes searched for a way out.

We were in a vault not much larger than my bedroom. I struggled to breathe against the hot, moist air. The only light, an orange haze, came from a crackling torch on the wall to my right. I shivered uncontrollably despite the heat. My hands clutched the sides of my head. I panted like a dog. *Jesus Christ, we're in a fucking tomb.* On either side of me, the walls were lined with crypts, the names of the dead etched into stone.

There were no windows, but there had to be a door. I swung around, my eyes racing in every direction. Where the hell was it? Where—

My heart came to a screeching halt. The doorway was behind the Overseer.

I couldn't hold back the tears. "Please, mister, let me go."

"You cannot leave… ever… Jimmy." The beast smiled so wide I thought his face would split open. He slid a skeletal thumb across the axe's blade.

Mr. Hanson squealed some more.

The beast laughed wickedly and mockingly patted Mr. Hanson's head as if to make a scared child feel better.

"I don't understand any of this." I wrapped my arms around myself. "Why are you doing this?"

THE OVERSEER

The Overseer's expression turned grim. *"Because it is time for you to take my place and become the Overseer. The spirits have chosen you. Oh, what a joyous time this is."*

"What are you talking about?"

"Oh, Jimmy—"

"Stop saying my name." A wave of hate burned my cheeks. "How do you know me?"

"Because I have watched you for oh so long and knew that you would come and accept your destiny." The beast took a step closer to me. I retreated. *"It is a great responsibility that you, like me, will undertake. I grow weary of my charge, and now pass it on to you, but, boy, you must freely accept this responsibility."*

"I don't want it." I dropped to my knees. "Please, just let me go."

The Overseer turned back to Mr. Hanson who shook his head wildly and wrenched his neck. He was choking on his own blood, bubbling up from between his lips. *"I believe you will accept once I give you the gift."*

I started balling. "I don't want a gift. I just want to go home."

The beast hefted the axe over Mr. Hanson. *"You said you'd kill him if you had the chance. I will do it for you."*

Mr. Hanson coughed and squealed louder, thrashing against his chains.

"No, I never said that," I cried out, knowing I had.

"Yes, you did, and so accept my gift as an offering for the sacrifice you are about to make." The Overseer swung the blade down. With a thud, it sliced into Mr. Hanson's guts, but the dull blade didn't cut all the way though. It lodged deep inside. Mr. Hanson didn't scream. He didn't cry. His head jerked back. His eyes locked on me. A tear slid down one of his cheeks. More blood gurgled from his mouth, spilling around him.

I pounded the stone floor. "No! No! No!" I hunched over. Spew flew from my mouth.

The beast just smiled and ripped the axe from Mr. Hanson. His entire body spasmed. His entrails splashed against the walls. Still, his eyes, twitching with what little life was left in him, remained locked on me. His mouth contorted in agony. I couldn't block out the sound of his gurgling final breaths.

The Overseer laughed. *"How do you like your gift? Shall we finish it, so that you can take my place?"*

With one more swing of his axe, he cut off Mr. Hanson's head. Like a ball, it rolled off the sarcophagus, bounced against the floor, then rolled until it stopped at my feet. I gazed down. His eyes remained open in a lifeless stare. Blood and puss bubbled from his exposed insides.

THE OVERSEER

He still had a tear on his cheek.

"Enough." I charged through the tomb, screaming wildly. Barged right by the beast. Slammed into the thick metal double doors with so much force I heard my shoulder pop and felt my bones crunch. "Someone, help me!"

The doors moved a little.

"Let me out!" I crashed against them a second and third time, ignoring the pain radiating from my arm to my chest and down my side.

The Overseer didn't try to stop me. He just roared in laughter. *"There is no escape for you, Jimmy. You've accepted my gift; now you must take my place. Become the Overseer."*

"Dad, give me strength." Lowering my head to my chest, I shoved the doors once more. They gave way. My chest exploded with hope. I busted through onto the cemetery grounds into the dead of the night. A white mist dragged across the drying grass, blocking my view to just a few feet in any direction.

I ran anyway, stumbling to my knees, then scrambling back to my feet and dodging past tombstones.

"Someone, help me!" I shouted.

There was no response.

The only sound was the Overseer's bellowing laughter following close behind. I glanced back, but the mist was like a wall hiding anything beyond it.

When I looked ahead again, I slid to a stop.

The mist parted, revealing a gathering of the dead. Their ghostly bodies hovered shoulder to shoulder. Rows of them. Unmoving. Wrapped in their burial clothing. Eyes vacant black holes. Mouths opened unnaturally wide.

"Welcome, Jimmy, we've been waiting for you," one woman uttered, her thin arms outstretched toward me.

"Jimmy, join us," a boy, one side of his head crushed, playfully sang.

"Jimmy, watch over us," an old man moaned. His suit was open, exposing his caved-in chest.

"Jimmy… Jimmy… Jimmy," they all chanted.

"No! God!" I buried my head in my arms and took off running, blindly hobbling into the mist. Gasping, Crying. Pleading. Snot rolling down my nose. "Mom! Anyone! Someone, hear me! Dad, don't let them take me!"

Thank God! Through the haze was the cemetery's entrance. The black iron gates were open. My heart did summersaults. *I'm going to make it! I'm going home, get Mom and get the hell away from here.*

I sprinted toward the gates, peering over my shoulder for any sign the Overseer or the dead followed me.

THE OVERSEER

Nothing crossed through the mist.

Gazing back at the entrance, I pleaded in silence for the gates to stay open. Tendrils of fear curled into my stomach, pushing me to run faster. I was almost there now. The gates still remained open. *Hurry!* This was it. I was going to make it. The beast couldn't stop me. The dead couldn't trap me. I wouldn't become... an Overseer. *Not tonight, fuckers.*

I reached the gates. Without slowing down, I crossed through to the other side. *Yes! I'm fre—*

I froze. My eyes blinked wildly in disbelief. My entire body numbed as if all my blood drained away. I dropped to my knees. Hands tore at the dry grass.

I was back inside the cemetery just outside the tomb I had escaped.

"No, it can't be." I lashed out, pounding my fists into the grass.

"Oh, but it is, boy." The Overseer spoke but didn't reveal himself. *"Do you see now? You must accept your fate."*

"Fuck that." I picked myself up and ran again, pushing past the dead who reached for me from their graves.

I reached the gates again. *Please. Let me go home.*

I crossed through... and was back at the tomb.

DARREN SIMON

Dropping into the grass, lowering my head into my hands, I let out a terrible shriek. The last tiny flame of hope inside my chest disappeared, leaving nothing but a cold, lost void deep in my gut.

I looked up toward the sky, blocked now by a ceiling of fog. "Dad, I'm so scared. Don't let them take me."

"Don't be frightened, Jimmy." The beast crossed through a wall of mist in front of me, slowly dragging his axe along the ground. The blade clanged as if it slid over a slab of concrete.

Still sitting in the grass, I lowered my eyes and tucked my legs into my chest. I couldn't bring myself to look up at him. I just stared at his muddy, worn boots, the tips and heels covered by blood. My head spun. It was so heavy, I just wanted to lay down and close my eyes. Dizziness took over. I couldn't think. I couldn't feel. The tears stopped.

"Boy, look at me." The Overseer softened his voice.

I didn't respond. I couldn't.

"Jimmy, I said look at me."

This time his voice was different. Familiar. But it couldn't be. My body trembling, I lifted my head... and gazed into another face. Gone was the decaying flesh hanging loosely from a skull. Gone was the twisted smile and black goo dripping from the beast's mouth.

THE OVERSEER

"Dad." I mouthed the word.

"Yes, son." My dad's face, as kind as I remembered, looked down at me. He had the same brown hair and large brown eyes that could make you believe everything, no matter how bad, would be all right. He smiled at me just like he used to with just the slightest lift of his lips.

I shook my head. This couldn't be right. "Dad, is it really you?" My heart raced. That tiny flame inside of me sparked to life.

"Yes, Jimmy, it's me." He bent down on one knee. He rested a hand on the axe handle and the other on his bent knee. He tilted his head to one side. "I want you to join me, son. I miss you so much."

I slid away from him. "Dad, I don't understand."

"Jimmy, I'll explain everything." He leaned closer to me. Extended a hand toward me. *"All I ask is that you take my hand and say you'll accept my gift, then all will become clear. And we can be together for all times."*

"Dad." I started to reach a shaky hand toward his, then recoiled. A moment of clarity returned. "No, you're lying. You're not my dad. I slid further away. "He'd want me to live my life. Be there for my mom."

My dad's face contorted. His brown eyes popped out of their sockets, replaced by the beast's yellow glowing orbs. His skin shriveled, half of it melting away to reveal the Overseer's skull. His lips twisted in a vengeful grimace. The beast stood, his skeletal body creaking with each movement.

I held back a scream. Started to crawl away on my hands and knees. Scrambling to my feet, I turned to run but ahead of me the dead hovered in silence, blocking my way.

The Overseer's heavy boots crunched through the grass behind me. *"You will replace me, boy."*

I swung around to face him.

He raised his axe. "Or you will—"

A blinding flash of light slammed into his axe, shattering the blade. What was left of it flew out of his skeletal hands and disappeared into the mist.

The beast shrieked.

I gasped. Dropped to my knees. What was happening?

The beast stomped toward me. "Who dares—?"

Another flash of energy smashed into his chest, driving him back. The beast reared his head and screamed wildly.

A beam of white light encircled me from above. I covered my eyes and peered between my fingers. I couldn't see a thing, but the light was warm, comforting like… my dad's hugs.

THE OVERSEER

"You will not take my son this night, Over-seer."

It was my dad's voice. My chest heaved. Lungs filled with air. Could it really be? Or was this another trick? "Dad, are you there?"

The light around me faded. In its place, my dad appeared beside me. He was translucent, bathed in the same white glow, but it was him. It had to be. He wore his formal police uniform, golden shield on his chest, and his white eight-point cap covered his head. He smiled down at me, then placed a glowing hand on my shoulder. I couldn't feel his flesh, but the touch was as warm as the light that had surrounded me.

"Yes, son, it's me." He winked just like he used to, then turned his attention to the beast. *"You're wrong, Overseer. His fate has not been decided. He's going to live. You made your choices, and this... duty... is your punishment. Not his."*

The beast laughed painfully. Black smoke still rose from his chest. Goo dripped from his mouth. His yellow eyes dimmed. *"Oh, he will free me and take my place. If not now, soo—"*

My dad raised a hand toward the beast. A blast of energy shot from his palm, striking the Overseer in his chest. This time, the energy punched a hole in his insides, then ripped through his back, crunching bone. Black fluid poured from the gaping hole, spilling around his boots.

The beast fell to his knees, coughing and gurgling up more ooze. His mouth dropped open. He moved his lips as if to speak but no words came. One more time, he looked at me and smiled wide. Then the yellow glow of his eyes faded into nothingness. With a final spit of black goo, the Overseer fell forward into the grass.

The beast lay motionless.

I stared wide eyed at his body, each breath racing from my lips. The weight pressing against my shoulders disappeared.

A soft breeze swept away the mist.

The dead dissolved into the darkness until only me and my dad remained.

I studied his ghostly face. "Dad?"

"It's okay, son." He placed both hands on my shoulders. *"You're safe now, but you and your mom have to get away from this place."*

"Dad… I need you. Come back to me." I couldn't hold back tears.

He shook his head. *"I wish I could, but you're stronger than you think. You and your mom have each other. You're both going to be okay, and I'll always be watching over you no matter where I am."*

THE OVERSEER

I took a deep breath. "Is any of this real? Is there really an Overseer, and why did he choose me?"

He nodded. *"Every cemetery has one. They're cursed souls for the way they lived their lives. To escape purgatory, they agree to serve as the undead overseers who watch over the deceased until they rise… or fall. It is a terrible fate, and I guess this one thought it could trap you and free itself."*

I tried to understand, but my mind was a scrambled mess. "He said he'd been watching me, and this was my destiny."

My dad lowered his head. *"He was lying to you."*

"But it's over now, right?"

My dad leaned in closer. *"Yes."*

"Dad, I have so many questions."

"My time here grows short, son, and we have to get you home to your mom."

"Dad, no."

"I love you, son. Always remember." With that, my dad's glowing body pulsated brighter and brighter, the radiance spreading out to engulf me. I watched him as long as I could until there was nothing but blinding white light.

"Dad…"

Finally, I was forced to squeeze my eyes shut.

DARREN SIMON

***

"Dad… Dad…. Dad!"

"Jimmy, wake up. You're okay. Wake up now. It's just a dream."

Those words came from my mom. My eyes shot open. She sat on the side of my bed, caressing my hair. Rays of sunlight crisscrossed into my room through my closed blinds. As I shook off the sleepiness, I became aware that I was drenched in sweat. My heart was beating so fast that my chest ached.

"Mom!" I pushed myself up on my elbows.

"That must have been some dream, Jimmy." She leaned in a bit closer, her hand still on my head. "You were screaming out for your dad, like you were terrified. I had the hardest time waking you up. Are you all right?"

"I… I don't know." I looked past her, scanning my room for any signs that what I experienced was anything more than a nightmare. There was nothing—not even a chip in the plaster where the beast slammed me into the wall. "Mom, what time is it?"

She checked her phone. "It's 10 a.m."

"What?"

"Jimmy, are you all right?"

THE OVERSEER

"I… I don't know." My head swirled as if lost in a storm. Had it all just been a dream? It had to be. But…

"Mom, we can't stay here." I climbed out of bed. I was still in my T-shirt and jeans.

A look of confusion crossed her face. "Jimmy, I—"

Her cell rang. She lifted the phone to her ear and answered, "Hello?"

I couldn't make out what the person on the line was saying, but Mom inhaled suddenly. Her face grew pale. She placed her free hand over her mouth. "I can't believe it. That's terrible. I was just talking to him yesterday when we moved in."

"Mom what is it?" I asked.

Her expression changed again. The lines on her forehead deepened. Her eyebrows wedged together. "Wait, I don't understand. How could that be? He hasn't known me that long. It doesn't make any sense." She paused as the person on the other line spoke. "Uh, okay, I can come by, and we can discuss it. And I'm so sorry for his family. Please let them know my thoughts and prayers are with them."

My mom gently dropped the phone onto my bed. Tears formed. "I can't believe it."

"What, Mom?"

"That was an attorney for the Hanson family." Her hands trembled as she spoke. "Mr. Hanson was murdered last night. His body was found outside his house this morning."

"What?" My legs crumbled beneath me. I collapsed into my bed. "No, it can't be. It was just a—"

"There's something else." She gripped my hand tightly. "Apparently, days ago he drafted up the paperwork deeding ownership of this house over to me. He left a note that he never wanted us to leave. Jimmy, we own this house now. I just don't understand. It doesn't make sense." She covered her glassy eyes with her hands.

I bit down on my lip until I tasted my own, warm blood. *It was just a nightmare.* I repeated that over and over.

For some reason, I inched over to my blinds. Holding my breath, I slowly opened them, then peered through the window at the cemetery.

A loan worker in overalls, his long hair covered by a baseball cap, stood among the tombstones, digging into the ground with a shovel.

At that moment, he stopped to look up toward my window.

And smiled wide.

BUT I WON'T DO THAT

Ric Wasley

He shielded his dark blue eyes from the final rays of the setting sun and as the last light tinged the western sky pink, then ochre and finally a deep crimson purple, his finger touched the button that opened the retracting steel louvres all the way.

The dusk settled over the rolling grass and bushes, fading into the dark pine and sequoia forest that stretched from his property all the way to the Big Sur California coast.

He took another sip of his favorite Croizet Cognac Cuvée Léonie 1858 and for the hundredth time sighed and regretted that he had not had the foresight to buy several more cases during all those years he had resided in France after fleeing the failed attempt of Austrian archduke Maximilian to become emperor of Mexico.

He sipped the 120-year-old perfection of vineyard and distillery and remembered.

That was during one of his "soldier of fortune" phases.

He'd finally lost enthusiasm for most of those romantic *Casus Belli* over the past nine plus centuries.

Although he had to admit he did sometimes miss it.

After all, when you'd been trained in every art of war from ax to sword to dirk, crossbow to longbow, and flintlock to M-16, it was natural to try and keep your hand in.

Besides, most of his forays into lost causes had ended in disillusion if not outright disaster.

His whimsical fling with being a southern cavalier in the Civil War had ended badly - as had the original one with the luckless Charles I two hundred years earlier in England.

He should have given up gallant gestures of Cavaliers, lost causes and chivalry then but hey - when you had forever to play with destiny you could afford a few mistakes.

And the desperate gayety of the doomed Confederacy in 1864 Charleston had certainly seemed the most genteel and amusing place to make them.

He took another sip of the velvet blend and smiled as he recalled one of the few romantic dalliances of that ill-fated last gasp of the Antebellum South. He savored another sip as he let the long-ago memory of Charleston's most enticing Southern Belle drift across the crowded shadows of his memories.

Sally Buchanan Preston, or "Buck", as she was known to her legions of admirers, was a girl of not just beauty, but of charm and wit with that measure of innocent flirtation that had had every male from beardless boys to gout-ridden politicians... and not less than a few generals, hopelessly enamored of her.

Chief of these had been the most feted but luckless of Confederate Generals, the newly appointed commander of the Army of Tennessee, one John Bell Hood.

Hood had arrived in Charlestown in July of 1864 and fallen promptly and hopelessly in love with the vivacious and beguiling Sally Buchanan "Buck" Preston.

Unfortunately for Hood, he, himself, had arrived one month earlier in June. And a month was more than enough time to entice the winsome Miss Preston into falling in love with him.

After all, when you'd had centuries to perfect your seduction techniques at the soft but knowing hands of some of the most practiced courtesans of Europe, it wasn't hard to charm any lass, no matter how flirtatious, from the wide-eyed, and somewhat naive world of North America.

Thus, when he and "Buck" had been introduced to the stiff and sweating Hood at a reception hosted by her best friend, Mary Chestnut, he'd actually told 'Miss Sally' to go and be nice to the awkward and tongue-tied cavalry general.

She had and within ten minutes the same buffoon who wound up leading thousands to their death at the Battle of New Market was hopelessly besotted.

So much so that before he left to begin his ill-fated command, he begged her to marry him.

She hadn't wanted to, he recalled, but by that time it was obvious to even the most dedicated and dim of observers that the Confederacy was on its last legs.

And since he'd long before learned his lesson about riding lost causes down to their sad but inevitable doomed conclusion - such as lingering too long on the walls of Constantinople while Memet's cannon had reduced them to rubble - he had already decided to resign his cavalry commission and return to Europe.

Thus, after a teary goodbye with the heartbroken Buck he advised her to say yes to Hood and try to grab herself a secure place in what would most likely be a very bleak Southern landscape after the war.

She had reluctantly taken his advice but later remarked to her friend Mary Chestnut that she only did so with the expectation that the luckless

BUT I WON'T DO THAT

Hood who'd been wounded in about every major engagement he'd participated in, was unlikely to survive to claim her.

He finished the last of the cognac, stood and stretched.

He couldn't recall if Buck had followed his advice to its logical conclusion and actually married the much-marred cavalier after the war but then again, he really didn't much care either.

That was one of the inevitable pitfalls of a heart (at least in the poetic sense) grown too jaded over the centuries. Women usually found him intriguing, witty, passionate, urbane and …dangerous.

With a few memorable exceptions he, more often than not, found them predictable, clingy, and as of late… interchangeable.

He shook his head. That sounded harsh, even to his own jaded ears and it was not as if the women he'd wooed and bedded were not also witty, alluring and exciting in their own right. Just not to him. At least not for very long.

He continued staring out at the twilight as the last stray beams of light faded down to a smoky, dark purple.

During his first century he'd been as brash, romantic and passionate as any young mortal man and had garnered his fair shares of lost loves and broken hearts.

Until he realized that hearts that could never die could never really break.

That blessing, or curse, was reserved for those who lived with the knowledge that all too soon youth and beauty would vanish forever with only roses on a tombstone to mourn their passing.

But how could you mourn something that never ended? Or find any solace in a love that time and nature would destroy in the blink of a cosmic eye?

If he was being as honest as he should, given nature and experience, he shouldn't even bother taking a lover anymore.

He often thought it was worse for the ones he lingered with the longest - the ones he developed an actual affection for. That was perhaps the cruelest of all.

Watching them watching him - watching them grow older and he not.

A beautiful woman reaching thirty, then forty and then the inevitable wrinkles and first grey hairs.

While he remained an unchanging thirty-two forever.

He reflected on his hundreds of loves over hundreds of years. The naive and knowing, The sweet and the sinister. The virtuous and the vain.

BUT I WON'T DO THAT

But they had all had one thing in common… they were beautiful, intelligent and fiercely independent.

That's probably what had drawn them to him.

In a world which often punished independent women, he encouraged it. No matter what form it took.

A duchess seeking some passion and intellectual stimulation from the role of the heir producing machine she'd been married into.

Or a poor, but ambitious country girl desperate for something more than a teenage marriage, a dozen children - with less than a handful surviving to adulthood - and an early grave for a body used up by thirty.

Those he felt with some satisfaction he'd saved from a lifetime of drudgery as he'd always left them with a fat purse when it had inevitably been time to move on.

And then there were those whose brains, beauty and wits he had helped to achieve the everlasting fame and independence they had so craved.

The fiery haired Elizabeth Tudor who'd come within a cat's whisker of losing her head before it could ever wear the crown.

He could take a small bow for saving her pretty white skin by persuading her to play the dutiful sister to Bloody Mary while she bided her time and waited until a small amount of poison could hasten that harridan's departure to her self-directed purgatory and clear the way for, "good Queen Bess."

Elizabeth did remember her debt and granted him an estate in the Lakes country which he'd used off and on until the post WWII taxes left it more trouble than it was worth.

The same for the Chateau in the Loire gifted him by one of his more scatterbrained conquests, Marie Antoinette Josèphe Jeanne, the newly crowned Queen of France.

There, he reflected, he had performed a real service worthy of the history books. Namely giving France a male heir to that somewhat shaky throne.

History had long speculated whether the 16th of the Louis couldn't get it up for his pretty if slightly dim teenage bride, or if he was 'shooting blanks'.

Well, I know but won't tell, he mused, but let's just say had the 'national razor' not cut off the Bourbon reign a lot of the succeeding monarchs might have looked like him.

Marie was probably one of his easiest dismissed affairs but when he learned of her sad encounter with Madam Guillotine, he did regret that an ocean stood between him and any chance of saving her from that sad and really, undeserved

BUT I WON'T DO THAT

fate. She never actually said, "let them eat cake". That was overhead at the card table in the green salon at Versailles. And he could swear that she never said it. Because he did!

He put the snifter precisely in the center of the tiny, inlaid table (another gift from Marie) and remembered.

There had been so many.

He hadn't set out to collect the vivacious, charming and famous - but so often that was the way it had worked out.

He picked up a silver snuff box chased with gold and inscribed *"From HRH Victoria to her Dear Count "X", For Impeccable Advice and Council"*.

Well, that, *"Advice and Council"* had been to give up her teen fling with him and marry Albert. So, for what it was worth most of the royal families of Europe owed him a tip of the hat as well.

It hadn't been all queens and nobility - there were spirited, sassy girls of every age. But some really stood out. And if they didn't have 2 nickels to rub in their worn aprons he couldn't have cared less.

He smiled at the memory of two little girls he'd taken under his wing for a year in the outlaw territories of the old American West. Little spitfires. Anna Emmaline McDoulet, better known as 'Cattle Annie" and her even younger accomplice, "Little Britches" (Jennie Stevenson Midkiff).

At an age when today's girls would have only concerned themselves with who was driving to the mall, those two were learning their fractions and sums by calculating the shares for the gang from train robberies.

As fun as that had been to be a big brother and mentor to the sassy pair they'd eventually wound up in a woman's prison in Framingham, Massachusetts where after finally growing out of their early season of rebellion they'd both grown up to be rather staid and unremarkable adults.

Perhaps that same delight in girls who were not afraid to take what they wanted from life was why he'd been so interested in the girls who'd been drawn to the new and revolutionary media at the turn of the 20th Century. The movies.

He'd come to Hollywood from the East coast in 1915 just in time to meet the winsome little Ingenue who'd just been crowned 'America's Sweetheart' by theater owner David Grauman…Gladys Louis Smith, known to fans of that day as… Mary Pickford.

At that time, she'd just become the theatre's highest paid star at the astronomical figure of $2,000 per week - at the time when one week of her salary would buy you a luxury home in an upscale neighborhood.

BUT I WON'T DO THAT

His romance with the winsome Mary had been the first but by no means the last he'd have in that town but inevitably he'd tired of her wholesome sweetness and yearned for more excitement.

So, in 1916 he'd returned to Europe where excitement had merged with terror in the slaughter pen of the First World War.

He'd been fascinated by flying and volunteered for the Lafayette Escadrille.

Obtaining a commission and a flying machine had been relatively easy as the attrition rate through death by arial combat and crashes had been appalling. Which of course had only served to add to his reputation of being uncharacteristically lucky in surviving crashes and wounds that would have killed any normal person.

Of course, he was no normal person. And being immortal didn't hurt either.

They also thought him incredibly daring for volunteering for night bombing and pre-dawn patrols that left him free to spend the rest of the daylight hours under a deeply shady tree or sampling the delights in a dark cellar club of Parisian cabarets.

It was there he'd met Margaretha Geertruida MacLeod, a Dutch exotic dancer and courtesan better known by her stage name, Mata Hari.

He'd spent a few delightful months with her in Paris and had grown fond enough of her to warn her that she was being used by the Deuxième Bureau who had persuaded her to use her considerable charms to entice the Kaisers Generals to share military morsels of pillow talk with her.

Alas she hadn't listened and when it all went wrong, as he knew it would, that same Deuxième Bureau had turned on her, had her arrested and later executed by a French firing squad in 1917.

And so, it had gone over the years and centuries, proving that from an immortal perspective, most love was impermanent, and all love was fleeting.

All but the current one…

***

Anya Tatiana Nikolaevna was not like the others he'd loved and grown bored with over the years.

There was something about her that was, well… different.

He'd had women as beautiful, as clever, witty, charming and even, sometimes, as hauntingly sad.

BUT I WON'T DO THAT

No, that wasn't right. It wasn't sadness so much as it was melancholy, perhaps tinged with wistfulness.

But not often. In fact, he only glimpsed it a few times. Out of the corner of his eye. When she was sitting across from him in some dimly lit cafe or on some remote cliff in the Big Sur overlooking the wild sea as the moon poked through torn shrouds of fog and mist.

At those few times he could swear she was feeling exactly what he was feeling. Almost as though she knew what it was like to be him and watch the centuries unfold. Ever changing while he never did.

But how could she really know? How could any mortal?

No, that was just another facet of her endless fascination for her that kept him returning to her with more curiosity than he'd felt since the night when Ann Boleyn confidently told him that she could, "most assuredly handle Henry." Well, she'd realized her error too late, just like poor Marie Antionette. Why did they never learn?

But he had the feeling Anya would not have suffered their arrogance and subsequent fate.

She was too ... observant, thoughtful, patient. As though she had been waiting for something all of her life.

And tonight, he intended to find out what.

He had first met Anya Tatiana Nikolaevna at a music club in one of his increasingly rare forays to the old music club part of the metro area two hours distant from the secluded estate.

He had always enjoyed music over the centuries. Everything from the Beatles, "Rollover Beethoven", to Beethoven in person.

He had held a box seat at the Paris Opera House as well as in Vienna.

But unlike so many of his kind who preferred to live in the past, as musical tastes changed with the times so did his.

Thus, he'd frequented Carnaby Street and Haight Ashbury in the 60's as well as 'Stadium Rock' venues in the 70's and 80's. And while not much of the current music trends excited him, he did still visit the more intimate small live music clubs whenever he was feeling particularly restless.

That was where he met Anya Tatiana Nikolaevna.

He was seated in a dimly lit corner near the brick back wall of the club, feeling only slightly annoyed that he couldn't get his preferred table in the *exact* back corner - because it was already occupied. By a girl. A young woman of perhaps twenty, certainly no more than twenty-two. And

BUT I WON'T DO THAT

because his eyes could see better in the dim light than most people could see in a spotlight, a very attractive one too.

She had long chestnut blond hair falling loosely over one shoulder while a long stray lock played peek-a-boo with her left eye. Those eyes were hazel-green and as he was scrutinizing her, she suddenly looked up and caught his.

She didn't gasp or start or turn away in a cold huff but merely gave him the briefest of smiles before turning back to the stage to applaud the singer finishing her song.

When she turned her attention back to him, she took a sip of her drink and leaning forward across her table, asked softly, "What is it that you find so fascinating in this corner? Is it me or the table?"

He smiled. "Both."

He had long ceased being circumspect of feigning his interest in a woman since the mistress of the Doge in Renascence Venice spent an entire year on tutoring him in the ways of courtly dalliances.

"You see, that's usually my table when I come here. But if I must lose it, I'm glad it is to someone so charming."

"Nicely done," She replied with a nod and tip of her glass.

"Former English major I presume… or perhaps French Poetry?"

"La vie est une fleur dont l'amour est le miel," he replied.

"Life is a flower of which love is the honey," She responded, then added… "La vie est un sommeil, l'amour en est le rêve."

To which he translated back, "Life is a long sleep and love is its dream." And added in a voice barely above a whisper, "How appropriate." Although he wasn't quite sure whether he was thinking of her or himself.

She pointed to the chair beside her and said in almost as soft a tone, "Since I appear to have usurped your spot, I think it only fair that I should offer to share it."

She elegantly gestured her left hand to the chair again and with an incline of her pretty chin said, "Sir?"

He scooped up his drink and brought it to the corner table.

Seeing the movement, the enterprising waitress sensed a pick-up in progress and knew from experience this usually resulted in expensive drinks being bought but her expectations were outdone when the solidly built man with dirty blond hair and a faded puckered scar on his

right cheek asked, "What is your best bottle of Champagne?"

BUT I WON'T DO THAT

That was a new one on her. In fact, she didn't even know if there was one, but not wanting to be done out of a prospective windfall she quickly replied, "Let me check. I'll be right back."

It must have been that her stars were lined up right because after being grilled by first the bartender and then the owner to ensure that the guy inquiring wasn't bullshitting or too stoned to know what he was asking, she was taken down to the wine storage area and shown a bottle that read; "*Salon Champagne Brut Blanc de Blancs Le Mesnil 2012.*"

"That looks like a nice one." She said happily. "How much is it?"

Her smile soon died when the owner looked at her over the top of his glasses and answered dourly, "$1,300 bucks."

Watching her dreams of a big tip flit away she asked, "Why in heavens name do we stock something so expensive that no one will ever buy?"

"Because someone did," He answered morosely. This was ordered for a guy who used to stop occasionally to meet 'business associates' for 'off-the-books', transactions. Sometimes he liked to entertain them in the styles they were accustomed to in the sunny climates of their, South-of-the-Border, home turf. Hence outrageously expensive champagnes designed to flatter and impress."

"But if he ordered it for a meeting, why is it still here?" she asked as they reached the top of the stairs.

The owner sighed. "Because on his way to the meeting… where he would have also paid me for it, he was diverted by some gentlemen who wished to discuss why his last two shipments had been increasingly light. That was the last that was ever heard of him."

As she started glumly back to the table the owner put his hand on her shoulder and whispered, "Listen kid, if you can move that bottle not only will you score a fantastic tip, but I'll stick an extra $100… no, make that$150, in your pay envelope."

So, she bucked up, raced back to the table, put on her perkiest smile and said, "Well, sir you're in luck. We just happen to have a very special bottle of *Salon Champagne Brut Blanc de Blancs Le Mesnil 2012,* down in the wine cellar.

She nearly fell over when the soft-spoken man with the scar nodded and said, "I suppose that's passable. How long will it take to chill it?"

He never even asked the price.

That night a very happy waitress went home with an extra $150 from her boss plus a

BUT I WON'T DO THAT

staggering $500 tip that made the final payment on her Toyota.

***

They talked until closing time and then he'd asked if he could give Anya a ride home.

At first, she'd demurred but he'd gently persisted.

"I would use the old trope of the city streets not being safe for a pretty young woman late at night but I'm afraid that it's no longer just an old trope. Sadly, it's become alarming true. The streets today are crawling with violent lowlife who in earlier days would have been trussed up on a gibbet at the crossroads." And he should know because he'd trussed a few of them up himself.

She smiled. "Don't worry, they never bother me,"

He glanced at her and thought that was probably true, but he wasn't sure why.

And that was another of the reasons he had wanted to prolong the evening.

"Besides," she said. I prefer to walk. I really don't like motorcars."

Motorcars...? That's an archaic choice of words.

But he smiled back and said, "But I don't have a *motorcar,* tonight. I've got my classic 1958

Harley-Davidson Duo Glide, Air-Cooled, Overhead Valve, 45 Degree V-Twin, 74 Cubic inch…"

She held up a hand and laughed. "Stop… You had me at Harley."

He drove her home.

She'd eschewed his offer of a helmet, preferring to let her long hair fly in the wind, and of course he never wore one - why bother?

They lingered in front of her old Spanish style stucco front apartment building, and he knew **she** was considering asking him up. But he also knew he couldn't go.

The sky was beginning to turn from black velvet to hints of grey and he'd have to crank the Duo-Glide up all the way if he was going to make it back before dawn broke.

So, he leaned forward and brushed her lips with his and as he did, she pressed something into his hand. He slid it into the inside pocket of his leather jacket and gunned away from the curb.

It wasn't until later when he changed out of the jacket whose thick leather collar and hood had protected his neck from the worst of the scorch marks, he'd taken with the first rays of the sun caught him racing down his long driveway, that he found the note and read it.

"Thank you for a wonderful, and one of the most interesting evenings I've had in many, many

BUT I WON'T DO THAT

years. The marvelous champagne brought back happy memories of happier times.

I hope we can meet again… Anya.

***

The note had also contained her cell, so he had called the next day and they had been seeing one another with an almost prosaic regularity reminiscent of times long past, for the past six months.

Over that time, he'd become more and more fascinated with her and more and more convinced that she was hiding something.

And tonight, he was determined to find out what.

Thus, he'd finally invited her here, for dinner, and arranged to have one of his private services pick her up at 5:00 pm. She'd texted back her acceptance a half hour later but asked if the car could pick her up at 7:00 pm rather than 5:00.

She probably wanted to freshen up after she got home from work he assumed and since whatever time they ate dinner was immaterial to him, he quickly texted back, "No problem."

That left him with about eight hours to kill which was good because he had other, less pleasant tasks to attend to before he could fully return his attention to the oh so very intriguing Ms. Nikolaevna.

And that task was not only not pleasant or charming… it was downright annoying.

Though there might have been a case to be made from the 'intriguing' perspective, 'suspicious' might have been closer to the mark.

It had all started about a year ago.

His old 1950s version biker leathers had finally given up the ghost and he'd opted for an early evening sojourn to a mid-size town about an hour away to find a replacement.

After completing his transaction, he found a nostalgic craving for ale in some road-house dive, so he dropped his kickstand in front of a local Country/biker bar down the block.

Big mistake.

The ale was non-existent, the beer was watery and when he ordered a bloody raw steak lightly seared on both sides, they brought him a piece of suet he wouldn't have thrown to the hounds in his Viking long house.

But the disappointment didn't end there.

Apparently, the huffy eyeroll of the frizzy-haired waitress when he sent back the food untouched had signaled her regulars that some snooty 'new guy' was dissing the cuisine of their 'homeboy' haunt.

BUT I WON'T DO THAT

Sure enough, while he was debating whether he should finish the tasteless beer or just leave, a barrel-bellied bear of a man shambled over and stood next to his table.

"Crystal says you don't like our food around here."

It was a statement, not a question.

He looked up.

The bear was big. Perhaps 6'3" or 4". Small brown eyes set in a broad face covered with an unkempt reddish-brown beard that tangled down to his chest.

He stared back at the bear.

The ox would have been laughed out of any self-respecting long house. Even a raiding party, soaked and starving from battling storms and gales after a 10-day crossing, had combed and re-plaited their hair and beards with silver beads and gold rings before a feast or going into battle.

After all... what warrior wanted to enter Valhalla looking like some slave or peasant?

Odin's blood! Have a little pride you slob!

He apparently had muttered that last bit out loud because the bear raised his bushy eyebrows and growled, "What did you say?"

"About what?" he answered.

Not being quite sure what he heard, he paused for a moment before repeating his original question. "About the food."

"Actually, I made no comment. I simply didn't care to consume it. But since you apparently are so interested that you can't wait for my coming Yelp review, the short answer is that since my motorcycle boots are in no need of re-soling, I simply can't find another use for what seems to pass for steak around here."

The bear leaned in. He could smell the sour fetid beer breath that also indicated that what was left of his teeth would soon succumb to periodontal disease.

"You saying our food sucks?"

"Well, I'm not saying that all of the food around here sucks but as it related to you and your health, hygiene and diet I would be forced to conclude, that yes - it does."

The bear straightened up blinking, obviously trying to filter through the words to see if he'd just been insulted.

Finally coming to that conclusion, he growled, "Git up."

"Why?"

"You know why."

"Let's for the sake of argument, pretend I don't. So, enlighten me. Fill in the blanks."

The bear was getting confused. Too many words. And he said so.

"You talk too much."

BUT I WON'T DO THAT

"So, I've been told. And by now less a personage as chief inquisitor Father Vincenzo Maculani da Firenzuola, in Rome in 1633."

The bear's brow furrowed.

"Who the fuck is he?"

"Not, "is", *was*. Who the fuck *was* he. After all, 1633 was rather a long time ago. But to complete your inquiry Father Vincenzo Maculani da Firenzuola was the chief inquisitor appointed by Pope Urban VIII, to charge an astronomer form Pisa with heresy."

Slowly coming to the conclusion that here was being royally screwed with the bear said, "What fuck you talking about?"

"Your statement. That I talk too much. I'm actually giving you corroboration straight from the Papal Legate who said those very words to my argument when I said in defense of one, Galileo Galilei... that the Earth did indeed revolve around the sun.

In fact, a week after the luckless astronomer was sent back to Pisa under house arrest a warrant came for me but by that time, I'd made my way back to Florence and the welcoming arms of a brilliant young artist, the charming and most beautiful, Artemisia Gentileschi."

He looked up and winked at the increasingly befuddled bear.

"Talented in *all* of the arts, I assure you."

That did it. The bear was done. No more mental jousting with a broken lance, the bear wanted to get down to it. And if he was being honest, that was probably what he'd been hoping for ever since the bear had shambled over. All the reminiscing about longhouses, longships, and raiding was making him nostalgic for the 'good old day's' and old-fashioned, uncomplicated head bashing.

"Shut the fuck up and git up." The bear had spoken.

"Certainly. Any particular order.?"

The bear didn't answer, he just swung one ham-sized fist down at the table.

But that was all he hit - the table.

Because as the befuddled bear observed the seat where the smart-mouth guy had been sitting was empty. And instead, a hand on his left shoulder spun him around. "It works better if you aim before you swing. Tell you what, I'm a sport. Here's something we used to do long ago - after the mead horn had made a few rounds..." He dropped his hands to his side. "You get the first shot." He winked. "Make it a good one."

The bear blinked for a moment and then with a roar wound up and smashed a tremendous roundhouse into the left half of the stranger's face.

BUT I WON'T DO THAT

He was gratified to hear the crunch of bone followed by a gout of blood from the smart-ass stranger's nose and mouth.

The stranger grinned through bloody lips and pushed the dangling tooth back into his gums.

"Not bad. You might have even made the last rowing bench on the longship."

He licked the blood from his lips, and it seemed to the confused bear that cuts and massive bruising were beginning to fade before his eyes. The stranger grinned again but now the grin looked more like a wolf's.

"Now it's my turn."

And before the bear could blink again, he was on the floor, curled up in a fetal position, trying desperately to draw a breath into lungs that had been emptied from a blow to the gut that he never saw coming.

He gasped and writhed, face purpling as he struggled to draw a searing breath.

The stranger leaned down and said, "We done here?" As he dropped some bills onto the table and turned to leave.

That was when he was hit with a long-neck bottle of Schlitz that broke against his skull.

"Apparently not."

Of course, the bear had friends. And now the local code demanded they get involved.

Oh well, the more the merrier.

It's not like this was his first bar brawl, or 10th, or hundredth, or…

"Nice to meet you gentlemen." He smiled and stepped towards them.

When it was over, he had actually paid the damage to the bar and had even given the pale faced, frizzy-haired waitress who instigated the whole thing a far better tip than she deserved… "Here you go, maybe invest in a personality," he told her.

In retrospect he was probably having too much fun and should have been paying more attention to his surroundings. Such as the little man in the far corner of the bar who hadn't moved a muscle during the entire affair. So, he hadn't given him much thought.

That had been a mistake.

***

He sat behind his desk and drummed on the polished leather top. He flicked open the pneumatic catch on the desk top humidor and picked up a thick Cohiba Beehive Cuban cigar, inhaled the mellow aged tobacco and briefly considered lighting it. He'd gotten damn near hooked on the things when he'd been navigator to Bartholomew Roberts as they scooped up more than a dozen French and Spanish ships during the summer of 1720. He'd also tried to cloth himself in the captured silks and jeweled waistcoats, but the dour Roberts had snapped at him to "take that foppish nonsense off" or he'd he threatened to tie him to the bowsprit and let him become a target for enemy gunners. He'd removed the finery, but Roberts had no objection to plundered tobacco, so he'd consoled himself with Cuba's finest.

He still fancied them occasionally but put it back in the humidity-controlled box. He needed to concentrate on first things first.

And the first thing, the immediate thing, was to deal with the threat that he had failed to recognize in that the bar.

The odd little man that he had finally identified as one Peter Henny. But deeper research had revealed that he had been Christened in 1968 Amsterdam as Pieter Henrik Helwig.

Why would a Dutch naturalized citizen Pieter Henrik Helwig be interested in him?

It had taken some digging through many Dutch and then German records that had been lost or damaged in the carnage of WWII but finally a light a dawned, when a very old friend in the Smithsonian in Washington discovered that one Georg Andreas Helping, a Lutheran pastor in Prussia nearly 300 years ago, had developed an unusual passion for prowling graveyards with silver crosses and wooden stakes.

From there it only took a few oblique leaps of logic to chase down and confirm that yes, old Georg Andreas Helwing had been nothing less than Bram Stokers inspiration for the vampire hunting professor Van Helsing in his ridiculous, perpetually annoying… and in his estimation, way too overdone Victorian novel, "Dracula".

He sighed. It was obvious that this strange, transplanted descendant had taken his old family legends to heart and had set out to reprise a demented old family preacher ancestor into a modern day, real life Van Helsing - Vampire Hunter!

All of which would be harmless as well as completely laughable were it not for the worrisome fact that said nutcase had the title of "Special Agent", printed on the laminated nametag that also read, "FBI".

***

Unfortunately, it wasn't until six months ago that he'd uncovered that little tidbit.

It was also six more months since his frolic in the bar, which he'd promptly forgotten about the following day. After all, when you've cleared out taverns in Kiev alongside the warriors of Sweyn

BUT I WON'T DO THAT

Forkbeard or saloons in Tombstone next to Cole Younger and John Wesley Hardin, mopping up a few overweight biker wannabes deserved to be forgotten.

But unfortunately, someone else hadn't.

Even worse, it took him almost six months to notice. And when he did it was only by accident.

His deadliest enemy over the centuries had always been his twin terrors of boredom and inaction. So late one afternoon on a fine early spring day in April he donned his leathers and fired up the Harley,

It was approaching 5:00pm and sunset was around six so he figured that as he was heading east his thick leathers including boots, gloves and an insulated black helmet with polarized and double tinted face shield should protect him from any stray rays that a turn in the road might throw his way.

He was correct and got to a small college town that housed many interesting shops along with the usual college bars which also boasted a bountiful collection of winsome young ladies as bubbly eye candy.

While lovely ladies had been plentiful in every place and time in his long existence, he had to admit that not being covered up with yards of fabric and crinolines made viewing them a lot more enjoyable in the past half century.

To be fair, many of today's girls would have a hard time competing with 1861's crop of Charleston Cotillion Belles, hoop skirts or not.

He paused and leaned back against the brick wall of a trendy pub filling up with yuppie couples that would soon be replaced with college types and slipped a slim cheroot out of his top pocket.

He opened his face shield just enough to slip it between his lips and lit it. The last rays of the setting sun bounced harmlessly off the shield, and he exhaled. When the smoke drifted away, he saw that there was someone looking at him.

And that was rather odd because most of the people out on the street were looking at, and commenting on, the beautiful springtime sunset.

Most people were looking west at the setting sun.

But not this person.

He was looking east - away from the sunset. And the only thing to see in that direction was ...him.

The final rays faded, and he snapped up his visor but when he looked around, the man was gone.

He looked for the man for the rest of the night and thought he spotted him with his back turned before a noisy group entered, and he was lost to view.

BUT I WON'T DO THAT

After that he deliberately engaged in his own personal 'spy vs spy', pub-crawl.

He was sure he'd caught glimpses of the man all night, but it wasn't until his last stop when the final place was flashing 'closing time' and the lights came up that he at last got a good look at him.

Apparently, the man was unfamiliar with watering hole protocol and was taken by surprise when the lights went from dim to bright with the panic time…last call to hook up, clarion call of, "Closing Time!"

For a few 'deer-in-the-headlights' seconds his dogged shadow was pinned like a grey butterfly by the glare, before he could pull his hat over his eyes and hastily exit. But that was enough. He'd gotten a look. A good look. And though the little man had one of those nondescript forgettable faces so perfect for spy work, he would not forget him.

That night when he got home just before dawn, he'd lowered the shutters and spent the better part of the day sketching the face that he had locked into his memory.

He could have used his cell phone camera, but he was quite a good artist. The talented young painter, and his lover, from Renaissance Florence had taught him well and he'd had close to four centuries be perfect it.

RIC WASLEY

When he was finished, he ran the black and white sketch through an AI program that colorized and sharpened it until it looked almost like a photo. Then he up-loaded it to search through all the known facial recognition programs, cross referenced through Interpol, multi-governmental files and just to be sure, the Dark Web.

That was where the hit came from. Which meant the little man was deep cover... very deep.

He'd known for some time that the FBI was a welcoming home for those with a political agenda or a personal ax to grind so it didn't surprise him to learn that the Van Helsing descendant was using the agency as cover to indulge his vampire hunting fantasy.

Though to be fair, it was obviously not a fantasy to him. But he still needed some excuse to put into his case file unless he was doing this completely off the books. And given the amount of time the man seemed to be putting in, he considered that unlikely.

So, then he thought... what is he using as my 'crime'?

Joseph Stalin who he'd met briefly In November 1905 had of course the blunt, utilitarian answer.

He'd been introduced by Lenin's wife Nadezhda Krupskaya, to the new delegate of the

BUT I WON'T DO THAT

Georgian Bolsheviks at the Bolshevik conference in Saint Petersburg.

As he recalled, Stalin was a repellant little reptile of a man, but he recalled one nugget of passing conversation that had stuck with him about the niceties of crime and evidence… "Show me the man and I'll show you the crime," he'd stated in that flat Georgian accent.

And that's what came back to him now.

The Van Helsing pretender would just make something up to open a case file and justify the time.

But what?

He'd certainly been careful to cover the tracks of his various incarnations and identities down through the centuries, but he also had to admit that with each passing decade it was getting harder and harder.

That was one of the many reasons he'd come to America. He'd grown tired of changing countries, estates and chateaus. And with the growing officiousness of European bureaucracy, he decided that the freedom and independence offered by the new world fit perfectly with his restless nature and desire to move through the centuries with as much anonymity as possible.

The vast untapped continent of North America had offered that for the past two centuries. Oh sure, there were censuses and tax rolls but there was always a new territory to the West where people had enough to do with staying alive to not worry much about a reclusive bachelor who lived far out of town.

Besides, unlike Europe, which was all about cities and estates, positions and ranks in society, America thrived on the archetype of the loner... the independent - the free man looking for elbow room and no interference from anyone.

And that archetypical persona of rugged, if aloof, individualism, had served him well... until now.

Because now, the centuries... both 20th and 21st, had apparently caught up with him to put an end to a millennium of obfuscation and anonymity.

Shit!

Now what?

And tonight, of all nights.

Soon she'd be here and the last thing he wanted was to lay his centuries of dirty laundry in front of her.

He chuckled to himself as he pictured the filthy woolens and salt-stiff furs he'd dumped before the boiling kettles stirred by his mother and sisters when he and his father and brothers had returned from a summer's Viking up the rivers of England and Ireland or France... laden with plunder but reeking of 6 months of blood, mud and North Sea storms.

His mother had taken one look and a longer sniff and consigned the worst of their clothes to the fire and the rest to boiling pots while threatening that if they didn't scrub their filthy skins raw with sand and birch leaves, she'd toss their ugly carcasses into the boiling pot too.

His eyes turned inward, and he saw his father and three older brothers drawn up around the central fire in the middle of their timbered hall on the rocky fiord north of Kattegat. His mother dishing out the rich meat from a freshly butchered stag. His two sisters Ana and Freya bringing trenchers of fresh baked rye and barley bread along with brimming horns of sweet mead and strong ale.

He smiled at the memory, still as clear and vibrant as that day that he later learned marked the ten centuries since the birth of the Christians nailed God.

He chewed his lower lip.

Even after a millennium his rage still burned as he remembered how in the darkest hours before dawn, he woke to find the hall in flames and the demon warriors hacking his family to pieces.

He had stumbled, naked, out of his sleeping furs, grabbed his ax and rushed to where his father and brothers stood back-to-back swinging long swords and axes at an increasing crowd of black helmed warriors.

The five of them swung, slashed and stabbed until they had a ring of at least a dozen of the tattooed visaged attackers crumpled before them.

Then the scores of warriors parted and an enormous man with black-inked elder runes covering every inch of his face strode through their ranks and grinned.

"Bjorn Iverson." He'd spoken to my father. "Sweyn Forkbeard, your lawful liege lord had waited in vain for your tribute from this summer's Viking. Why have you not paid him?"

"He may claim that title as the son of Harald Bluetooth," he spat, "but claiming does not make it so. We asked for his aid, but he gave us not a single oar, sail or sword for our venture." He shifted his longsword in his hand and growled, "So we owe him what he gave us..." He flipped his sword from his right and to his left and pointed the tip towards the giant... "Nothing."

Instead of being angry the giant grinned.

"Then we will take your tribute in flesh - torn from the bodies of you and your sons and the sweet softness of your wife and daughters."

My father lunged at him, but the big man caught the blow on his shield with his left hand

and with his right ran my father through with his boar spear.

He didn't make a sound but whispered one word to us… "Fight."

And we did. But we were three teenage boys against two dozen seasoned warriors. One by one my brothers fell to sword blades and spear points until I was left bleeding from a dozen wounds, my back to the fire, in the middle of our blood-soaked hall.

I could barely lift my ax and now the warrior band was playing with me - taunting me.

"Come stripling," the big man boomed. "Throw down that useless ax, beg for mercy and we might let you live to be catamite to slake the lust of the pervert Franks or Ottomans when they have tired of you mother and sisters."

They all burst out laughing.

He held out his hand for my ax.

I let my hand fall and the ax hung loosely from the braided leather strap around my wrist.

Then as he reached out grinning, I pulled the haft into my hand, swung it overhand in a forward arc and lopped off his right hand at the wrist.

He bellowed in pain, falling back and clutching the spurting stump and while they were all stunned and staring, I dodged through their massed ranks and out into the cold night air.

RIC WASLEY

As I ran towards the pines, I heard him scream from behind me, "Draugr! Run him down."

I darted into the forest and ran faster than I had ever done but soon heard something heavy crashing through the brittle branches behind me. I dodged and wove but it was no use. I heard a hiss at my shoulder and the next thing I knew powerful talons closed over my shoulder and dragged me down.

I was on my back and pressing my body into the forest floor was a beast of a man with a narrow face with pointed ears, enormous blood red eyes and slavering fangs. The dripping teeth were inches from my throat, but I still had my ax looped around my wrist, so I took a frantic grip and swung it down with all my force on the beast's head.

I heard the satisfying crunch of bone and the creature fell off me and laid still.

I raised myself to one elbow and got slowly to my knees. I needed to go back - to try to rescue my mother and sisters.

I took a shaky step back toward the hall and heard a twig snap behind me.

I turned and could not believe my eyes. The creature was up and walking toward me. The rat-like skull still showed the massive gash from my ax but even as I watched, the wound was closing. The bone became smooth, and the furry skin knit. I backed up in disbelief, The thing grinned.

BUT I WON'T DO THAT

And then it came for me.

In a sudden rush it was on me and in one motion clawed and ripped the ax from my wrist and I was on my back once more.

This time the sharp, pointed incisor teeth sank into my shoulder and slavered up to rip out my throat.

I screamed in terror, but my father's words came back to me - "Fight!"

In a last desperate attempt, I tore my heavy silver Thor's hammer amulet from my neck and rammed it deep into the beast's left eye.

The creature gave a hideous shriek and left up howling, running in circles and foaming at the mouth until it careened into a massive pine and collapsed.

After a minute or two I was able to get up and find my ax.

Then I knelt over the beast and with one soul searing chop, severed its head.

***

After that, he recalled, he collapsed and lay unconscious for a day and a night.

He should have died but he didn't.

That one brief bite of the creature leaked something into his blood that saved his life.

It was a small taste, but it was enough - for the time being.

***

When he was able to make his way back to the hall, he found nothing but smoldering embers.

His mother, sisters, honor and much of his sanity was also gone.

He only had one thing left.

Revenge.

***

He was startled out of his reverie by the 17th century Bavarian chimes that he'd brought from Europe when he bought the place in 1892. At first, they had been on a bell pull but when electricity had finally made its way to the county, he'd seen no reason to forgo the mellow tone simply because Edison had allowed mankind to replace the tug on the bell rope with the press of a button.

He got up. She had arrived.

He'd sent a car for her, but it had come back empty with the message that she'd be along shortly at her own pace, her own time and in her own way. He liked that.

He assumed she had her own car but when he opened the door, he was surprised by what he saw pulled up on the white gravel circle under the porte-cochère.

He looked at the car and smiled down at her. "My god, you drive a Bentley."

She smiled back and stepped up to the marble threshold. "A 1961 Bentley S2 Drophead Coupe conversion, if you want to be precise."

He laughed. "Not only beautiful and charming but a 'gear head' too."

She glanced back over her shoulder. "I saw it in a London showroom window and couldn't resist." She smiled wistfully. "My father always was fascinated by fine motorcars. In fact, my little brother had begun a collection of little lead and tin models, but…" She trailed off and looked sad. "He never got a chance to drive one."

He opened his mouth to ask why but a look at her face told him this was a topic for another day. He left it there.

In a moment she shook it off.

"So please," she said spinning around like a Russian ballerina, "Give me the tour. This place looks like it's got a lot of history and if there is one thing I know, it's history."

"I'm rather fond of it myself," He smiled trying to keep the irony out of his voice.

Thus began a most pleasant few hours.

He showed her the place that he'd bought at auction from a land speculator who'd gambled beyond his means and had afforded him the opportunity to create the kind of sanctuary reminiscent of the hill forts, then castles and finally manor houses, that had sheltered him in Europe.

He still retained many of those European properties but after wars and revolutions had rendered them not as secure as he would have liked, this remained one of his favorites.

After touring and chatting he invited her onto the back terrace to watch the moon rising over the purple pines.

He was about to embark on an inane but safe set of polite conversation topics when she scanned the tree shrouded road, then abruptly turned and asked, "Are you expecting someone else?"

Thrown for a moment he shook his head. "No, why?"

She looked back toward the dimly lit ribbon of dirt road and said, "Because I think I was followed."

***

The man who had spent his life in single minded pursuit of a goal that fell somewhere between obsession and derangement adjusted his Zeiss Victory SF 10x42 binoculars and zoomed in on the French doors of the estate's back patio.

The precision German optics that had once allowed the Wafen SS to zero in their field artillery and mortar fire, brought the patio and the glass window whose steel shutters had just opened, into sharp relief.

He smiled. When he'd ordered the first pair of these superb optics the bean counters on the 7th floor of the agency had kicked it back with a snarky note that $7,000 was too much to pay for surveillance equipment, when Army procurement could provide standard issue for $4,000.

He'd returned them without a fuss and then re-bought them on Amazon for $3,000 and hidden them under the innocuous, all-inclusive catch-all of, "Tracking tools."

He refocused the Zeiss and the figures standing in front of the dimly lit room sharpened into clarity as if they we no more than 10 meters away.

He watched as they chatted, seemingly without a care in the world as he unpacked the SOUND SHARK Long Range Microphone - Equalized XLR Kit and set it up.

Within minutes he was able to zero in on their conversation just in time to hear...

"Are you expecting someone else?"

"No, why?"

"Because I think I was followed."

***

Shit!

He'd been so careful.

It must have been those clowns from the field office before he'd noticed they were following too close and ordered them to hang back at least a mile. He'd obviously made that call too late, and the damn girl must have spotted them.

He lowered the Zeiss and rubbed his eyes.

This was going to make things harder - much harder. But not impossible.

He took a black walnut case with brass hinges out of his coat pocket. He clicked the small catch and opened it. He gazed at the hand-crafted dueling pistol nestled in the molded green velvet and ran a finger down its barrel.

It was time.

He picked up the pistol, poured 110 grains of fine black powder down the barrel and picked up a half oz round ball.

He rolled it between his thumb and forefinger admiring how it shone. Pure silver.

He wrapped a linen patch around the ball and rammed it home with a short walnut and brass rammer from the barrel's underside and stuck a brass priming cap under the hammer.

BUT I WON'T DO THAT

Then he slid his great-great grandfather's primary weapon for hunting Christendom's abominations into his belt.

He was ready.

***

He looked at her quizzically after her declaration and was just about to ask, "Are you sure?" when off the northeast, illuminated by the first light of the rising moon, he saw a twin flash for only a second but it was enough to recall him to a memory of a mountain trail in the Balkans when he'd been fighting with Titos partisans and seen that same flash from the binoculars of a Wafer SS Mountain Division - just before their MG42 machine guns had sliced through his entire company and sent them all tumbling into the gorge below.

He'd lost an eye, three fingers and most of his right foot. It had taken him close to 3 months for them to completely grow back. He was in no hurry to repeat the ordeal.

She was right. She had been followed but it was obvious that they had only targeted her to get to him.

He sighed. It was time to move.

Again…

He glanced at the rising moon. Yes, it was time… But not for at least another hour. There were a few wispy clouds drifting across it. Maybe they'd increase and bring a little more darkness.

He could afford a little more time for a drink and to learn more about this prescient young woman who he was beginning to suspect was not as young and innocent as she appeared.

He turned back to her and said, "Thank you. You may be right, and I'll deal with that in a moment. But first tell me more about yourself."

She turned her head slightly. "More..?" She looked back thoughtfully. "What more do you think there is to learn?"

He smiled. "I have a sense of people and I sense with you that there is a whole lot more than meets the eye."

She sipped her drink and returned the smile.

"That's funny because I had the exact same impression of you."

He smiled back. And you wouldn't be wrong but as I am also a gentleman of the 'old school', I believe in letting ladies go first. So…"

For a full minute she didn't say anything. Finally, she moved over to the couch in front of the fireplace and sat down. She took a long pull on her drink and closed her eyes.

"My childhood was wonderful. We were such a close and loving family. My mother and father and my three older sisters and our dear little brother. Summers at our retreat or on Papa's yacht. The fall and winter in the city filled with balls and parties…"

She opened her mouth and gave him a sad, wistful smile. "I know it's so hard to imagine that world now, but back then…" She trailed off.

"You probably think I'm silly and sentimental."

He shook his head.

"No, I also think a lot about…back then."

She looked at him quizzically for a moment before continuing. "And it went along that way until war, and unrest and then uprising and riots - and suddenly, there we were. Fallen from a life of ease and privilege to despised and reviled prisoners."

Her hands balled themselves into fists.

"Until that night - That horrible night. The night they dragged us from our beds and herded us into the basement."

And suddenly he knew. It seemed impossible but there could be no doubt…

She looked up at him fiercely.

"The night that they shot my mother, my father, my brother and my sisters … and me!"

***

She told him everything.

Much he had suspected but not the final twist. And certainly not what she asked of him.

He lit a fire, and she relived that last night when her world changed forever. "They thought we were all dead. God knows they had fired enough bullets into us before the district Commissar, who was only slightly less drunk that the rest of that rabble, ordered a halt. Not out of mercy but concern he would run out of bullets if he had more counterrevolutionaries to dispose of before the next allotment of ammunition from the Peoples Committee of Armaments arrived.

So, his oafs tossed our bodies into an army truck and drove us into the forest where they dismounted the truck and began to dig a large hole. "

Her voice was monotone, her eyes flat and dark. She continued. "I lay there. more dead than alive, as the blood of my late family congealed around me while I continued to wonder why I was not yet in heaven with them. Had I been bad? Was God going to curse me to stay in Bolshevik hell forever. I only wanted to die.

But I didn't.

My left arm had been shattered by a bullet and my right shoulder pierced so it bled profusely but somehow, I was still breathing. But I knew if the Bolsheviks discovered that, I would not be for long.

BUT I WON'T DO THAT

So, when they tossed my limp, bleeding body on top of my family's I gritted my teeth and didn't cry out.

It was then that I had my only stroke of fortune - if you could even call it that.

The drunken Cossack murderers decided that they needed a break from their labors and gathered around the truck where they took out foul smelling cigarettes and cheap, reeking vodka.

It was then, when their drunken attention was focused on booze and cheap tobacco, that I crawled out of the hole and into the forest.

I don't know how far I crawled, bleeding and half conscious, but the next thing I remember was a pair of dirty brown peasant valenok boots in front of me and a raspy voice in a thick accent saying … "Well, Zozka, what have we here? A wounded dove with a broken wing."

"*She* had found me."

***

She paused and looked up at him… waiting.

Finally, he acknowledged what he had suspected but did not quite believe it until now.

"That is an amazing tale, Anastasia. Or should I say, Grand Duchess Anastasia Nikolaevna?"

She nodded with a wry smile. "Yes, but not since July 17th, 1918."

She drew a breath, but he knew what she was going to say before she said it.

"The night I died and was reborn. Almost."

He was puzzled for a moment, but it confirmed something else.

He needed her to continue so he nodded and said, "Almost a millennium after my own death."

He watched her while he took a sip of his drink and then asked the question that had been bothering him since the night they met.

"I've always suspected that you were one of us…"

She started to speak but he held up a hand.

"But there is also something about you which is… different from those of our kind."

He slowly swirled the amber contents of his glass and continued. "Almost as if you were something in-between the undead and the living. Not alive but not quite yet dead."

He inclined his head as if in apology and said, "But I suspect you were about to get to that before I so rudely interrupted you. My apologies 'Grand Duchess Anastasia'."

As soon as he said the words, he regretted them.

"Sorry…"

BUT I WON'T DO THAT

"Anya," she supplied, her mouth crinkling in an ironic smile, "I've found that name to be far less… dangerous."

"Anya." He smiled back. "But please, continue. How did you survive? I assume you must have been partially turned before the 'true death', but I was never aware of any of our kind in the wilds of Siberia. Who was your 'maker'?"

Her green eyes stared past him, into the dark forest of Yekaterinburg on that night more than a century before.

"I never learned her name because she never told me. I staggered along behind her for who knows how long before I lost her in the dark. Finally, I could go no further.

I sank to my knees wishing only to join my murdered family in heaven.

It was then I saw a faint light from a ramshackle hut. I thought it might be a wood cutter's hovel or charcoal burners hut and I tried to cry out for help but could barely make a sound. I would have cried for sorrow and frustration, but all of my tears had drenched the earth where my family lay, and I had no more.

So, I laid my head down the frozen dead leaves and pine needles and closed my eyes to join my family when something wet and warm touched my cheek. I opened my eyes to some sort of wolfhound towering over me and that's when I heard the words, "Ah Zozka, she has come. Our little wounded dove with a broken wing.""

"I learned later that the people in Yekaterinburg called her а ведьма. Or as you would say… a witch."

He nodded. "We called them a völva, and every village had one. They were the daughters of Freyja and could help us back to life or ease us into … death. I also met one. - though I suspect not as gentle as yours."

Her eyes bored into his.

"But yours must have been more powerful than mine. Because while the old woman who found me and by the blood of her and her wolfhound saved my life and made me what I am today…" She looked down and paused before continuing in a low voice… "neither living or dead… or the living dead. She lacked the power to do one or the other."

She paused and he knew, instinctively, that she had more to say.

"And that brings me to why I'm here tonight."

He said nothing.

She watched him for a moment before continuing. "And yes, I know that you know, that there is something more behind my accepting your invitation.'

He remained silent, anticipating what she would say next. And he was right - but also wrong.

BUT I WON'T DO THAT

She took a sip of her drink and regarded him from beneath her long blond lashes that had never seen cosmetics.

"You know that I am 'like' you, but not 'of' you and your kind."

He felt at once confirmed but still conflicted.

He had surmised as much but could not quite understand it.

So, he said so. "That's why you perplex me. You seem to be an amalgamation of mortal, vampire and... lycanthrope?"

She responded with a sad smile.

"Yes. My 'Vedmak' was little more than a very old lady who had some of the undead blood passed down to her indirectly but not enough skill to know what to do with it. And the hound? Who knows - a forest strain of lycanthropy?"

She shook her head but continued.

"Thus, she could not 'make' me as I believe you were 'made' nor completely rejuvenate me from the brink of death where I hovered. She only allowed the hound to feed on me and lick his saliva into my bleeding wounds as she fed me a potion of forest herbs and her own blood."

She drew a deep breath.

"And *that* is why I am here. I'm tired of being a bastardized hybrid of the undead and the cursed living." She was right. For he saw that she had drawn in a heaving breath - Something he had not done for a thousand years... She continued.

"That's why I've come to you. I want to finally take my place in your ranks - The ranks of the immortal undead."

***

The man in the dark trench coat tapped an icon on his tablet and noted with satisfaction that the last of his handpicked team had arrived and moved into place.

He typed the code words on his screen and watched as each of the icons changed from yellow to green in acknowledgement.

The "Go-Code" had been given and confirmed.

It was time to move.

***

The room was lit by moonlight and firelight.

"I'm not quite sure I follow you," he said.

"You don't follow what I said?"

"Perhaps not completely." Though he was afraid he did.

"Then *perhaps...* I need to be more direct."

"In what way?"

BUT I WON'T DO THAT

"In a way that cannot possibly be misconstrued. A way which demonstrates that I am not here merely to take and give nothing in return."

She got up from the opposite chair in one fluid motion that was both determined and vulnerable.

She stood before him and regarded him with wide, sad eyes that had seen much and expected little.

"I'm not offering this as flattery, or even a form of recompense or inducement, but just to show you that I have been drawn to you since the first moment we met."

"Why?"

"Because I saw someone across that table who was as lonely and bereft as I have been.

And I thought that maybe, just maybe, we could be less lonely together."

She took his hand, and he stood up and they walked through the dark house with the dimly lit corridors to the only room where there were no electric lights - No TVs or internet.

Only candles and a large stone fireplace. A room where everything remained in the 10th century. The place where he slept when the sun he could no longer tolerate burned.

His bedroom.

***

He came fully awake.

Not that he had been sleeping.

What passed for sleep among his kind occurred when the sun was high - a strategy of survival developed over the millennium - providing a time of rest if not slumber.

This was not either. Merely a rare spell of physical and emotional satisfaction and yes... restoration and reflection.

A rare time in a very long time where he was able to recall past events with something akin to fondness rather than ennui and cynicism.

A feeling different than the thousands of seductions and affairs that had entertained him while not fulfilling him over the past millennium.

He had ironically, in this new era of open and casual sexual potpourri, begun increasingly to withdraw and become almost celibate. Not by design but from a feeling of the same boredom induced by a surfeit of too much rich foods and elegant spirits.

Or in the words of an old rock song from a half century earlier... "The Thrill is Gone."

Until her.

Anastasia - if it really was her. And the more he thought about it the more certain he became.

She had rekindled something in him that he had not felt for a thousand years.

BUT I WON'T DO THAT

Not since Revana... his shield maiden woman.

Her name meant 'Raven' in the old Norse, and she had been swift as a raven in battle, with fiery red hair and flashing green eyes. She had fought in his band but was the woman of an older chieftain until in a battle against the clans of Erin she'd received a sword slash that left one side of her face disfigured in a permanent scowl.

Her chieftain, who already had two wives and numerous slave concubines had callously informed her that he no longer had any interest in her warming his bed and told her she must find other accommodations among the war band.

But the other warriors - who had long courted her for her skill in battle and beauty, callously followed their chief's lead and it looked like she would have to sleep in the Meade Hall with the slaves and servants.

A beautiful and brave warrior woman alone because no one wanted her. But he did. He had long admired her but despite his reputation as a rising young warrior, he'd not yet had the following to challenge a chieftain for her.

But now...

He came to her as she was packing her small bundle and spoke. "Revana, I would be honored if you would share my bed and stand beside me in battle."

She turned the slashed side of her face to him and said, "Do you do this from pity?"

In answer he kissed the livid scar and said, "No." Then he turned her head to the flawless skin and kissed her other cheek and looked at her full on. "I do this for respect and yes, I think, love."

He had never regretted that choice.

Over the years they had fought side by side and loved and laughed together.

And when his life had hung by a thread - she had saved it.

They had been raiding on the Scotti coast when a sword thrust had pierced his mail and leather breast plate and left him close to death. The retreating crew of his dragon ship wanted to leave him, but she had instead bribed and threatened an old woman to take them to a cave in the highlands where it was rumored, they still practiced the blood magic of the Druids. There, in a cave, she had somehow induced an ancient shaman to share a few drops of a bloodline that was old before the sacred bluestones of Salisbury plains had been raised. The blood that brought earthly death but gave eternal life.

Neither of them had known it at first. They were too happy.

He recovered - seemingly overnight. And they went on to become an invincible pair in battle, winning much honor and gold and silver.

BUT I WON'T DO THAT

Eventually they left the war band, bought a farmstead and settled down to have children. But none came.

He did not know then that immortality comes at a price.

And that price included not just the denial of children, but of a love to grow old with.

He had to watch her age, grow frail and die.

He buried her with his own hands and set out into the wide world - alone. Always alone.

***

He looked at the young woman resting beside him.

Was that why he was drawn to her? Because she was alone - like him?

She opened her eyes and said, "Yes."

"Wait - you knew what I was thinking?"

She nodded.

"How?"

She shrugged, "I suspect whatever it was that happened to me in the forest more than a century ago."

She sat up in bed and rested her chin on her knees.

"You see I learned later that there were others like you… but none like me. I never saw the old woman again nor the hound and the blood magic that saved my life and condemned me at the same time. A freak even in the shadow world. Some sort of cross between a vampire and a lycanthrope with perhaps some ancient forest magic thrown in.

All that I do know is that I can sometimes see into a person's very being… soul if you like and know what they are thinking."

"But then you are immortal like me?"

She shook her head.

"No. And that is what I'm asking of you.

You see I'm caught somewhere between the living and the undead.

My life has been extended but it is not unending.

I age - slowly - very slowly, but I do age."

She bit the inside of her lip. "As near as I can calculate it is at about one tenth the rate of mortals so that after a century, I've aged but a decade.

But I have aged. And will continue to do so. Unless…"

"Unless?"

"Unless you can make me like you. Unless you can give me a home, someone to share with and be with instead of a universe of one. Alone."

He could see the longing in her eyes. She was speaking the truth. That was really all that she wanted and that was what he wanted too. But…

BUT I WON'T DO THAT

"I'm sorry. I can't."

"But why? Yes, I know we've spent little time together, but I can feel the connection, don't you?

Or is it that you don't - or feel that you can't ever love me?"

"No, that is certainly not it.

And yes, I think I can love you.

And yes, I would do anything for love…"

He stared back at her and slowly shook his head, "But I won't do that."

***

There was another sound coming from the long driveway to the house, the footsteps on the gravel followed by a pounding and a shout. "Open up!"

Moments later came a reverberating thud and the sound of the wide oak door crashing inward.

They had arrived.

***

He grabbed her hand and started to pull her up, but she resisted.

"Why?"

He looked back at her.

"What do you mean, "Why"?"

"I mean why won't you do it?"

"Why won't you make me like you - something whole - not halfway in between one thing or the other?"

"We don't have time for this."

He went to the walk-in closet, opened the concealed door set into the dark walnut paneling and stepped inside of a room filled with camera monitors and banks of flashing hard drives.

He checked the closed-circuit cameras. The men were on the first floor. He clicked on a bank of switches and a steel door at the end of the hall clanged shut. It would slow them down, but it would also pinpoint their location.

No matter. He'd run out of time - and it wasn't the first time, so he was always prepared. But that preparation left no room for error, so they had to move.

Now.

She was already dressed when he came back and it took him less than a minute to slip into a black T-shirt and jeans, a pair of heavy black engineer boots and a thick black leather jacket with a hood.

As they moved into the hallway, he immediately smelled the acrid stench of burning metal and saw the steel door at the end of the hallway emitting sparks around the locking mechanism. They had cut roughly halfway through a semicircle around the lock plate and would complete the cut in no more than minutes.

"Com' on." He pulled her by the hand as he led them down a side corridor to a small elevator that served the four floors of the house plus the basement and garage.

He pressed a button and the door slid open. At the same moment a crashing sound came from the other end of the main hallway. They were through that door too. He had only seconds.

He reached inside the elevator and pressed the button for the first floor but withdrew his hand before the door closed.

"Maybe that will throw them off the scent for a few minutes."

"This way." He took her hand and led her to what looked like a broom closet but once inside another concealed door led down to narrow stone stairs.

"We should have just enough time but it's going to be close."

***

And it was.

By the time they emerged into the garage level he could already hear the elevator whining down from the upper floor.

At first, he considered the black Hummer 4x4 with the dark tinted windows but then discarded it for the motorcycle as that could take them to any number of caves or remote fishing camps where even 4-wheel vehicles couldn't go.

He heard the elevator doors open and the footsteps of a dozen pairs of shoes shuffle out. They weren't taking any chances.

He slid onto the motorcycle seat and fired up the big machine.

He pressed the key fob in his jacket pocket and the heavy double door of the garage started to rise but before it had gotten three feet off the ground a burst from a Heckler & Koch MP5/10 erupted, smashing the garage door's driving motor and rendering it inoperable.

He'd have to find another way but first they needed to get out of the line of fire.

He turned to take her hand as three 9mm slugs stitched a bloody line across his back slamming him forward into the handlebars.

It hurt like hell, but he knew he'd heal.

However, he didn't know if she would. The odd mix of blood she had taken had saved her life and slowed down her ageing, but would it heal her from the kind of firepower that was ranging against them right now?

He didn't intend to find out.

BUT I WON'T DO THAT

He could feel the bleeding holes in his back already beginning to close, so he pulled her sleeve and said, "Get on."

"No."

"No? Why not?" Another burst of rounds slammed into the concrete next to his right foot.

"Because if you won't make me as you are, then I cannot spend eternity with you. And if I must leave you, I'd rather do it here and now. Let these Bolsheviks do to me what those a century ago failed to do."

"You really feel that way?"

She nodded and said in a voice tinged equally with bitterness and sadness, "Yes. You said that you loved me but while you claimed that you would do anything for love… you also said, "But I won't do that."

He had. And he had meant it but after all these years could he really face another millennium without love and companionship?

Could he leave her stranded between two worlds? And while able to walk in both never be long to either? Did she really want to give up the daylight to become a true creature of the night in exchange for spending it with him?

Would it truly be enough?

Did she really know what she was asking? To never see the sun again. The bright blue sky. swim in a sparkling sea or a sunlit meadow. To savor the smell of morning dew. To fill her lungs and… breath?

How could he be a part of taking all that away from her? That was why he had said no.

Did she realize that? What would she give up? Was that truly what she wanted - To spend eternity with him in the world of night?

He stared back at her but her, but her eyes never wavered.

Finally, she whispered, "Yes."

He stared at her.

Had she heard his thoughts?

"Yes," she said again.

He opened his mouth but before he could speak, a bullhorn behind him blared. "Get off that bike and put your hands up!"

He looked in his rear-view mirror and saw the man in the dark raincoat raise a square metal tube to his shoulder… RPG - rocket propelled grenade. They weren't playing around. A bullet he could remove and heal from - but being blown into little pieces…? No.

"On the count of three I fire. One, two…"

He stared back at the man and screamed, "Three!" in defiance, then gunned the bike forward in a screeching wheelie. He'd have to time it down to the millisecond. He heard the swoosh of the RPG and spun the big bike in a tire smoking turn that reversed direction as the partially closed garage door exploded into flaming fragments.

He skidded to a stop in front of Anastasia and took her hand. She said nothing, only watched his face staring into his eyes.

The smoke was beginning to dissipate, and he could hear the sound of running feet and a voice calling for another RPG.

It was time to move - for the last time.

He motioned to her to get on.

She didn't move - only stared at him with the same question in her eyes.

There was only one answer. He looked back at her, his expression unchanged.

Then the corners of his mouth softened, and he nodded, "And yes, I would do *anything* for love..." he grinned. "Period."

She smiled, kissed him and climbed on behind him.

He put the growling machine into gear, and they roared off into the deep black night... together.

DEATH STALKS DARDEN PLACE

Francesca Quarto

The visit was planned with an out-of-the-blue phone call.

"Saw where you moved to my neck of the woods, so thought I'd just jump in the car and drive up to visit you guys at the new place. You're less than a few hours away now buddy."

Neil quickly switched to speaker on his cell phone since his hands were busy with unpacking.

"That's great, Stan. I can use your help moving the heavy stuff around in the house." Stan assured Neil he was in the best shape of his life.

"Will you make it a turnaround trip or stay overnight?" my husband asked, his eyes now searching my face for a reaction.

"A few days, three max. I'm having my house fumigated for an ant invasion, so I can use that time to help move you in and catch up with your life since frat days. I'll have my laptop and can work from anywhere but the bathroom. How many of those have you got in that palace? The way you described it in your text makes it sound like the Playboy Mansion. Hope it's as much fun!"

His ridiculous comments were followed by a loud laugh. Neil gave a soft chuckle, shrugging his shoulders at me. He knew I'd have no objections to an old fraternity friend visiting, but we'd only been here a few days, and barely gotten through a third of the boxes. There were small mountains of unopened boxes of new stuff too, bought anticipating our much larger house. I sighed and bobbed my head. A minute later Neil was getting ready to say goodbye, joking about not picking up any hitchhikers along the way.

"Only if they're as hot as your wife!"

I groaned loudly. I'd only met Stan a few times at various college functions and was underwhelmed at his attempt at acting cool. My opinion remained unchanged, and I heaved another sigh.

"Oh, by the way. I'll have some company along for the trip. My dog Finn will be with me, if you guys don't mind. He's an Irish Wolfhound, sort of my emotional support dog. A sweet guy, mostly sleeps all day."

"Aren't those dogs over a hundred pounds?" Neil asked looking back at me, his eyebrows mirrored my own, raised in alarm.

"Yeah, but like I said, he's very mellow and no trouble. See you guys tomorrow. Hasta la vista baby!"

DEATH STALKS DARDEN PLACE

"Neil, Stan isn't really bringing his dog along on his visit…is he?"

"You heard him, love. Finn is a sweet dog. Mostly sleeps. It's only for a few days and he'll be a big help with the unpacking."

"The dog too?" I mumbled.

"Hells bells, Neil, it will be November before we find our winter clothes in this maze! How can Stan help?"

Neil moved closer putting his arms around my waist.

"You worry too much, Laura. It'll be fun having the first visitor to our new home. I'm going down to the wine cellar to pull some bottles," he added, sounding like the owner of a B&B preparing for guests.

I took the narrow servant's stairs at the back of the kitchen to the second floor moving to the only finished linen closet of the two upstairs. Pulling sheets and a comforter for a guest bedroom, I was reaching for towels when an icy shiver ran through my body. My outstretched arm froze like the claw in a toy merchandizer machine. I was consumed with an overwhelming feeling that this visit would bring something deeply disturbing, even…evil… into our life. I shook my head mumbling angrily to myself for allowing absurd thoughts of dark entities to scare me like a child afraid of the bogey man. I blamed the creaky, shadowy mansion for the creeping feeling I couldn't shake. Something bad would soon be here.

***

Next morning Neil left me his phone while he showered, in case Stan called. When he did, he announced loudly he was parked in our driveway. He sounded slightly annoyed I hadn't noticed, as if I should have been keeping watch like he was visiting dignitary!

I'd been unpacking my adoptive mother's old China in the formal dining room, placing each delicate piece on the table. The wide surface was as dark as a pool of black water, seeming to stir under the twitchy lights of the old chandeliers. Twelve chairs, cushioned in blue velvet, lined a gilded wallpapered wall, with the sideboard gleaming across from me after my careful polishing.

Fighting annoyance at the interruption, I ran to the foyer, pulling the heavy wooden front door open in time to see Stan hefting a stuffed duffle bag from a Land Rover that looked like he'd driven through a swamp. He was shutting the passenger door with an elbow, while trying to control the huge gray Wolfhound that leaped out. I opened the door wider, inspiring Finn to break away, galloping toward me. Stan struggled to hold on to his bag while futilely grabbing for the dog's collar.

Stunned by this explosive entrance while trying not to get trampled, I froze when Finn fixed his golden eyes on me. A chill ran through me as Stan yanked on the dog's collar shouting "NO, Finn!"

"Hey, Neil my man! You must have heard my grand entrance with my buddy."

Finn was drooling…or salivating…straining against Stan's hold on his collar.

"The big guy just needs to get used to being around new people and he'll be as sweet as a bunny, right boy?"

Finn sat down in answer, proving he could be around Neil and me without going into attack mode. Neil gave the dog a tentative pat on the head as he picked up the dropped duffle.

"It's great you can help out for a few days and catch up, Stan."

It was questionable if Stan was astute enough to pick up Neil's emphasis on the word 'few'. He leaned down to whisper in Finn's ear. The dog answered with a single thump of his tail.

He smiled up at Neil. "Sure thing, fella! What are old frat buddies for if not to help a brother out?"

"Stan," I said, forcing a smile. "We have a huge backyard, and it's completely fenced. Why not let Finn," his golden eyes fastened on me

"…uh…romp around outside for some exercise, while you bring your bag up to your room."

"Yeah. I figured the wrought iron fence went around the back, when I drove through the double gate. That fancy script D on the gates is very classy by the way," he said, totally ignoring my suggestion.

He went on, "This place must be at least two-hundred years old! Ivy crawling up stone walls, wooden shutters and iron framed front door…*gargoyles* for Pete's sake…and it's huge! How many rooms does it have?"

"Well, it's actually only one-hundred- thirty-years old and there's more rooms than we need, right Laura?" Neil said with another strained smile in my direction. I told Stan half the rooms were closed and unused for now.

"We'll give you the history over dinner," I added, hoping to get him and Finn out of the foyer.

We'd been in our new place for four days. We counted twenty-three-rooms and discovered from the estate attorney, Matthew Brimmer, it was a near replica of a centuries-old monastery in Ireland. The only exception as far as we knew, was that a large part of the cellar held vintage, cosseted wine bottles instead of bodies of deceased monks.

My birth mother's great, great grandmother, Geraldine, and her new husband, Victor Darden, had it built in this remote part of the upper peninsula of Michigan after returning from their honeymoon in Europe. The lawyer said it cost twenty million by today's accounting, with much of the materials and all the stained-glass windows shipped over from Ireland and Italy. Victor was fabulously wealthy, though Mr. Brimmer, whose family of lawyers represented the Darden interest for over a century, was unclear on how he created his vast fortune. He said Victor was a man of mystery and had the money to hide whatever he wanted hidden.

The story he shared surrounding Geraldine and Victor sounded like a fairytale. Geraldine traveled extensively after her first husband's untimely death, leaving her a rich and childless widow. While touring Ireland she fell in love with the dashing Victor Darden, who surely impressed her with his vast estate and unique manor house; an ancient monastery striped of any Christian icons and converted into a magnificent mansion. After a whirl-wind courtship, they were married there in a civil ceremony, Victor being a confirmed atheist. Returning to the states to please his new wife, Victor purchased and cleared a huge swath of land to build a mirror image of the monastery right down to duplicate gargoyles at the four corners of its roof.

Victor and Geraldine had two daughters, eighteen months apart, Susanne and Madalyn, whom they called Maddie. The girls lived a sheltered, almost cloistered life, ironic since the original monastery served as Abbey Dorney in Ireland centuries past.

Maddie married first but died in childbirth along with her infant. Susanne married soon after, giving birth to my maternal grandmother, Lucy. Susanne's husband Lucas succumbed to a strange stomach ailment before Lucy turned two. Rumors at the local pub hinted at poisoning by my great-grandmother, who according to household servants loathed her husband's very presence. The story eventually made its way to the local authorities, but because of Victor Darden's standing in the small community and his vast business holdings, hints of rat poisoning in a coffee cup went uninvestigated.

Susanne's daughter Lucy grew up under the shadow of suspicion that hung over Darden Place. When she reached sixteen, she escaped from the dark stories and whispered accusations to be with her love, Davey, the seventeen-year-old son of Victor's chauffer. It is likely Lucy was pregnant when they ran away together. In time my birth mother was born and given up immediately for adoption through the midwife's contacts.

DEATH STALKS DARDEN PLACE

The romance between my maternal grandparents cooled under the weight of poverty, and Lucy ran away again, but this time from her lover. She returned to Susanne's open arms, and the luxuries of Darden Place. Victor and Geraldine never knew about the birth of my mother, but Lucy did tell one truth; she and Davey never married.

Upon the death of Victor Darden, Geraldine planned to leave the entire estate to their daughter Susanne. When Susanne died of Influenza, Geraldine was forced to leave the wealthy estate to the only known heir, her disappointing, reckless granddaughter, Lucy.

Over the years following her inheritance of Darden Place, Lucy became a determined recluse, haunted perhaps by the memory of handing her newborn infant to strangers fifty years earlier. Toward the end of her life, she presented her attorney with a hand-written will, instructing him to track down the secret daughter. The Brimmer firm hired a private investigator, who, after several months of searching, discovered my birth mother died at twenty-six from tuberculosis leaving behind her own daughter, me, the last of the Darden bloodline.

At the time of the dramatic upheaval in our lives, we were renting a cottage near Grand Travis Bay, taking the summer off before Neil began med school, and I finished my masters. We'd been living off a small allowance from Neil's trust fund when I tore open the envelope that would change our lives forever.

The letter from Matthew Bremmer & Associates was tucked into a pile of mail forwarded to the cottage. I read it once, handing it to Neil. It stated my maternal grandmother, Lucy Darden, left her fortune and estate to her last living heir. Bremmer & Associates had "*unquestionably identified*" me as that heir.

***

We were still trying to figure out in what wing of the medieval designed mansion the movers put our winter clothes when Stan showed up with an Irish Wolfhound the size of our car. I was busying myself with putting together lunch for all of us, when Stan came into the kitchen.

"Wow! Where's the scullery maid? This kitchen is enormous! I can't get over this place's ancient look and feel…right out of a history book. But at least you have some modern amenities like your bathrooms. I don't think you'd be too happy with a chamber pot!"

I gave him a look, hoping to discourage more of the same comments, and went on to change the topic.

DEATH STALKS DARDEN PLACE

"It's going to be a pretty boring lunch since we haven't shopped yet. Hope you like ham and cheese."

"I ate along the road, but you and Neil should chow down while I unpack."

He smiled broadly and left me holding the mayo, watching his broad back recede down the gloomy hallway. The electric sconces were pretty, but not very effective lighting in the high-ceilinged rooms.

My mind wandered as I took out the plates. I was curious where Stan found a place to stop. Restaurants were non-existent for miles on any approach to Darden Place, same for grocery stores. There were no other residents within miles. We'd only seen a curious fisherman out on the lake the whole time we'd been here. He didn't stick around when Neil shouted hello, just lifted a hand and lumbered away.

Darden Place rose like a stone fortress out of a densely forested area of the peninsula, isolated for miles in every direction with the bay at its back. I shrugged off my curiosity and set out our lunch. It dawned on me that Finn wasn't with Stan. "Must have finally put him out in the yard," I mumbled as I washed the sandwich knife feeling an odd relief. I love dogs and we'd be getting a rescue pup as soon as we settled in, but there was something unsettling about the wolfhound, something in his golden eyes that came close to an uncanny intelligence.

Later that evening, sitting at the long kitchen table, we finished off the remnants of a reheated chicken dinner with baked potatoes and a tossed salad. Finn lay by Stan's chair. After a glass and a half of wine I nearly forgot he was there. Neil pulled another bottle of wine from our beautiful stainless-steel refrigerator, the only modern thing in the house. It replaced a large, dingy white antique model, its motor sprouting like a head on top. It was shoved into a shadowy corner of the kitchen for now, looking like a disgruntled spirit.

Neil topped off our glasses. The fine crystal seemed absurd sitting on what was obviously the cook's workstation; deep knife scorings and stains covered the newly scrubbed surface of the heavy oak table. I looked over at Stan's plate noticing Neil and I were the only ones eating.

"Sorry about the leftovers, Stan. Hope the wine makes up for it," I said lightly.

"Don't worry about me. I'm just fine and the wine is very good. By the way, Laura, I've been meaning to ask you. There's a plaque near the front gate attached to a huge boulder that reads 'Darden Place.' Was that your maiden name before you got hitched to my friend here?

"Actually, it's an old family name on my birth-mother's side. I was adopted, so no."

DEATH STALKS DARDEN PLACE

Not wanting to go into long explanations of family history, I stood up with Neil's plate and mine and headed to the sink.

"Honey, how about showing Stan the back door to the yard so he can put Finn out for a while? I'll clean up in here and you guys can go catch up. You deserve a break, Stan, after Neil worked you so hard this afternoon."

I was drying the last glass when the hairs on the back of my neck stirred. A chill ran down my spine like ice water. In that moment all my suspicions were confirmed. A low growl rattled the bay windows in the small breakfast nook. Slowly turning my head, I saw a patch of white fog spreading across the rippled glass. Finn stood on his hind legs, paws planted on the wide stone ledge, dark red eyes staring back at me. I moved toward the window, our eyes locked. I took a deep breath and touched the pane with the palm of my hand. Now I was certain of what I had feared from the time they arrived.

I'd been found.

"You'll be sorry you came here beast," I hissed.

I knew he heard my warning. His upper lip curled back in a snarl, exposing long incisors, thick saliva forming black spots onto the stone.

***

When we met with the estate lawyer upon arriving in Travis Bay, he handed me a bulky, yellowing envelope addressed to *'The Last Darden Heir.'* He explained it had been locked in the office safe since my great, great grandfather Victor Darden handed it to the firm's founding partner Jules Bremmer, over one-hundred years ago. He waited for me to open it, but I slipped it into my purse to his obvious disappointment. Neil smiled over at me, understanding my almost compulsive need for privacy.

After I read it alone, I told Neil it was just a bunch of birth and death dates of various family members, and the deed to Darden Place. I handed that to him to take his mind off the other item in the envelope. A long letter written on stationery bearing the Darden family crest, a wolf on two legs with a sword through its heart, was tucked behind the deed. In Victor's tight scrawl, it detailed my true heritage and explained, at last, some of my physical abilities and sharp instincts. He said as the last Darden I would take my place as *The Hunter.* The history of this oddly named position read like horror fiction. I could almost hear Victor's voice echoing off the high walls of Darden Place.

"Our ancestor, the first Victor Darden, lived in a small Irish village during the reign of Henry VII.

DEATH STALKS DARDEN PLACE

He carried many secrets into his great age of eighty when he died, but only one became woven into the fabric of life of his descendants, including mine, and now, yours.

"As a young boy, Victor was savagely attacked while checking traps for rabbits in the forest surrounding his village. He was being badly mauled, screaming for help, when an old woman holding a wooden staff sprouting red leaves at the top, stepped out of the green shadows. She shouted a stream of foreign sounding words, hammering the staff onto the ground. The beast sprang to its hind legs, running like a man on fire into the dense woods.

Young Victor woke later that night in the crone's hut. She looked almost as frightening as the beast that attacked him, with her wild gray hair, stooped back, and rotted teeth, though she gently tended his wounds with herbs and salves of her own concoction. Two more days and with her help he could sit up and feed himself the awful tasting gruel she insisted he eat to complete his healing. Of that, he was amazed! Deep wounds on his chest and arms were reduced to pale pink scars.

The young boy was in the small hut for many days, listening wide-eyed to the old woman's stories about the creature that attacked him. She swore him to secrecy before telling him she was a 'woodland witch,' a 'guardian of the forests, its many creatures and any human passing innocently through the woodlands'. The beast that attacked him was not one of these, but a monster. Victor heard it named by the witch and would name its kind himself many times in the years to follow. Werewolf!

When the pink scarring was gone, Victor prepared to return to his family. As he stood at her door, the witch revealed that beside healing his wounds, she had given him significant gifts. He would have the ability to sense a werewolf hiding in plain sight as a man or animal, and he now possessed the power to destroy it. She confided she was nearing the end of her mortal days, and with her passing, he would become the hunter of these monsters. She warned him these evil beasts would not vanish from the earth, and would have his blood, and that of his descendants, impressed upon the collective memory of the pack after his attack. She told him he must pledge his life, and that of his bloodline, to destroy these perverted creatures as long as one Darden survived.

For people like Victor, living in Ireland in the early fifteen-hundreds, life was filled with dark times. In the years following his own attack, there were violent murders of farmers savaged in their fields, and poor villagers living in and around County Kerry, found torn apart in their own beds. When Victor was seventeen the local armorer was attacked, and his store of weaponry taken by local peasants determined to protect their families. Soon after this incident, the post of Royal Werewolf Hunter was created by leave of the monarch's appointed mayor, Thomas Burmingham. It was said, the king laughed at the absurd idea of hunting mythical creatures as he called these shifters, but he agreed something needed to be done to quiet the fears and quell the rising unrest among the peasantries.

Young Victor knew his fate was to take up this post, and even with the promise of high bounties awarded for proof of each kill, no other villagers came forward. During the ensuing years Victor uncovered what he believed to be the last pack of werewolves, hiding in a monastery, wearing the assumed persona and brown hooded robes of the murdered monks. Victor had the witch's gift, an uncanny feel for dark powers. When he purposedly sought a night's rest there, he knew the impostures would take it as an opportunity to slay him.

Victor prepared for the inevitable attack. When the false monks fell upon his bed with teeth and claw, they tore open a straw-stuffed blanket. The Hunter sprang from the shadows and used his sword like a scythe. Heads fell like rotted pumpkins from a cart. Victor wiped out most of the pack, but two escaped into the night. When studying the faces of the dead shifters, Victor noted a strong family resemblance among six of them, thinking a whole family must have been taken into the pack.

Posters placed in public spaces declared the series of murders had been solved and the murderers caught and punished. The story put abroad identified the killers as lunatics from a prison asylum. Though the savage murders stopped, the local people had questions and suspicions about the two Byrne brothers who vanished from their prosperous mill, leaving behind two nephews to run the business. Rumors flew that the brothers were truly werewolves, responsible for the vicious attacks, basically ignoring the public notice about rampaging lunatics."

****

And this is where I come in. By the time my great, great grandfather Victor Darden moved with his bride Geraldine to America, the stories of werewolves had slipped into the same story books as those of Leprechauns. Victor was likely relieved of any duty as The Hunter. The Irish countryside had been peaceful for many centuries, but time merely covered truth like the

DEATH STALKS DARDEN PLACE

ubiquitous grey dust that covered every inch of our new home when we first arrived.

When Stan's wolfhound barged through our front door, something inside of me recoiled. As Finn brushed by me, his body gave off unnatural vibes. Discernment of such subtleties was one of the gifts I suspect I inherited from the first Victor Darden. The other gift the Woodland Witch endowed the young Victor and his progeny with was even more important, the power to destroy the beast.

Stan and Neil were drinking beers, watching a Lions football game on our Christmas gift to one another last year; a seventy-inch TV. It looked like a time-traveler sitting on the exquisite antique table surrounded by the ornate furnishings in the dining room. Relieved to have them occupied, I worked out my strategy to kill the last of the Byrne brothers. I had to admit posing as an Irish Wolfhound was clever. I believed Stan had been duped when one of the beasts shifted into Finn's shape after destroying the poor dog. Stan never guessed he was traveling with an evil doppelganger.

I theorized the last Byrne brother, upon learning my great grandfather sailed to America, was driven to follow him by the blood lust for any of the Darden line, as predicted by the Woodland Witch.

FRANCESCA QUARTO

Following the Persian carpet-runner, frayed at the edges by time and vermin, past a sitting room overlooking the gardens, chocked with tall weeds, its statuary and fountain draped in thick moss, I made my way to the library. The walnut paneling held an inviting warmth, with hundreds of books filling the shelves along two walls. The floor to ceiling bay windows created a curved niche on the back wall, where a beautifully carved writing desk stood inside the inviting space.

My senses sprang to life as I moved toward the glass alcove. A tingle ran through my hand when I touched the green shade of a reading lamp. Laying it on its side, I peeled off the black felt from the base. Reaching in I removed three glass vials from snug slots built into the hallow interior of the base around the electric cord. One was empty, the others filled with a dark yellow liquid. I slipped them into a pocket of the vest I wore over my shirt to fend off the constant chill of the old house.

Victor likely secreted them away before he and Geraldine traveled to their new home in America. He fully expected to be tracked here from Ireland by the werewolves with a taste for his blood, burning like a brand inside them. There were possible unexplained murders reported around the Upper Peninsula after my great grandfather's arrival with Geraldine, while the beasts remained unsuccessful in finding him. I needed information if I wanted to remain the last *living* Darden.

Scanning the array of books was overwhelming, and there was no time to look anyway. I ran back to the kitchen grabbing my laptop off the counter, returning to Victor's desk, the lamp back in its proper place. I turned it on. Scrolling down a list of book titles about this area, I stopped at *Dark Mysteries of Michigan's Upper Peninsula, by Stephen Clement.* According to a brief biography on Wikipedia, Clement was a young policeman from a Detroit precinct before moving with a widowed sister to the UP. He was well acquainted with the families in the sparsely settled area, serving as a Sheriff's Deputy, and then Sheriff until his strange death. His book was posthumously published by his sister, a year after Clement was found *"savaged by wild animals on the grounds of the Darden Place mansion while performing his duty as an officer of the Law."*

Stephen Clement was not the first victim found on the densely wooded estate, which was likely what led him to Victor. He might have been investigating the horrific killings of three hunters at the time of his own death. My gut told me he was killed by the last Byrne brothers. I sat staring at the blue-white screen, not seeing the words, but thinking about Finn. I snapped the laptop closed.

My time for strategizing was nearly over as the shadows lengthened across the floor and climbed the bookcase like soot-colored moss.

Back in the kitchen I pulled the two vials from my pocket. I held them up to the light. The yellow liquid was thick and dotted with what appeared to be tiny black seeds. I wondered how I'd deliver the poison to the impostor wolfhound. Looking in the direction of the bay windows, the sky had lost the dull light of early evening. I heard Neil and Stan laughing as they started back down the hallway toward the kitchen. Not knowing if the dog was with them, I made a hasty exit through the kitchen's back door, into the small mud room. Afraid a light would be seen, I listened like a thief in the dark as they came into the kitchen talking about the game. Neil said something about a sandwich. His next comment was muffled as he rummaged in the fridge. When something heavy hit the floor, I bent over to look through the old fashion keyhole. Looking down I saw Neil lying face down near the open refrigerator, bread and wrapped meats scattered nearby on the black and white tiles. My hand covered my mouth for fear my scream would escape. I couldn't see the huge dog through my tiny periscope, but Stan leaned into view, grunting as he lifted Neil under his arms. I picked up the sound of low groans. *Neil is still alive* I thought, breathing in a sob. They moved out of view entirely, the thumping of Neil's shoes echoing like hammer blows in the silent house. Desperately afraid for my husband, I caught the legs of the wolfhound as it followed.

When I was sure they were gone, I switched on the lone light bulb hanging overhead, unlocked and opened the door, grabbing a jacket and a small mag-light before bolting into the night. I was certain Neil would be used as bait to lure me into a trap if I tried to save him. If I vanished from the mansion, Stan and the hound would have to hunt for me, giving me time to set my own snare.

I looked up to see a star speckled night sky spread like a heavy quilt, tufts of gray-white clouds brushing the face of a full moon before floating by. *This is their time then.* I no sooner had this thought than the silence of the woods was shattered by a howl from the very depths of hell. My battle would soon begin and my only weapon, vials of liquid against claws and teeth and the strength of ten men. But I was the last of the Darden Werewolf Hunters, how could I lose?

***

The guest house on the estate was the only place I could think of where the shifters could make their transition into werewolves. A good distance from the manor house, I followed the remnants of a field stone pathway discovered on our walks, and knew it led directly there. The flat rocks were mostly obliterated under dirt and springy moss that muted my footsteps as I hurried. The outstretched branches of the trees gave them the sinister appearance of looming wraiths. This part of the estate woodlands had been undisturbed since my great, great grandfather's day, and the tight spacing of the trees gave me an odd claustrophobic feeling.

The guest cottage sat on what was left of cleared land making the rest of the stone trail visible through weeds and stiff grasses. The small house was covered with ropey vines crawling like black snakes up the brick walls and through broken windows. A carpet of dark moss clung to the tiled roof and brick chimney. Wearing this close-knit green and brown mantle, the house almost looked like a living creature.

I approached from the side to look through a window. The path I followed hadn't been disturbed, but that didn't mean the beasts hadn't already been here. Standing precariously on a pile of rotted split logs, I looked into the dark interior of the cottage. With the break in the green canopy of trees, the moonlight peered over my shoulder lighting the broken, worm-eaten furnishings. As I stood on tiptoe for a better view, Stan's muffled voice coming from behind nearly made me fall. I ran behind the cottage peeking around the corner at the visitors.

"Now, brother, when we kill the Darden woman, we'll make it look like 'er pathetic husband did fer 'er in a rage. There's no one 'round these parts fer miles an' it will be easy ta fool the local constabulary."

That wasn't Stan's voice, was it? He had an…Irish accent!

He's one of the brothers that survived at the monastery!

Neil was still alive! I heard a loud snuffling sound and then a second voice.

"We'll split up ta hunt 'er down, but we shift *now* brother. She is close by. I can smell 'er fear."

All went still. Guttural snarls and grunts erupted followed by cracking sounds like bones being broken and bodies being reshaped. A minute later a terrorizing howl, quickly joined by a second, shredded the silence of the forest with a hellish sound. I held my breath waiting for them to move in my direction when the howling ended. Taking the vials from my pocket, I was about to pull the stoppers when one slipped from my sweaty hand. My heart was hammering wildly as I searched, my fingers finally brushing the cool glass. I looked around, finding a discarded piece of the spear-like post from the iron fencing. I had a second weapon. I slipped both vials into my pocket, creeping around the corner of the house toward the front. They were nowhere in sight, but a heavy musk scent hung in the damp air.

Hoping for a place to ambush one of them and even the odds, I approached the front door. It hung from a single hinge. About to step closer, a very human moan came from somewhere inside. *Neil!* This is where they stowed him until they could pin my murder on him. If one brother shifted back to Stan's persona it would be easy to set Neil up as the depraved killer.

I moved sideways through the narrow opening of the front door not wanting to risk it squealing loudly if I opened it fully and stepped into the front room. Before searching for Neil, I had to be certain the brothers were searching the grounds for me. My ear pressed to the outside wall, I heard a low growl.

One beast stayed behind!

Would he come inside?

He must have heard the same groan I did and decided to investigate. I shifted to stand by the torn door frame into the deep shadows where the moonlight was blocked by overhanging trees. Hands gripping tightly around the iron post, I was ready. I nearly dropped the make-shift spear when a hairy arm, ropey with muscle, grabbed the dangling door, and with a guttural snort, hurled it past my head into the room. The beast stomped into the room, its heavy muscles rippling under a taught pelt of black fur. It stopped abruptly, listening. It was long enough for me to come up from behind. It must have smelled my sweat and spun around.

From somewhere in the Darden genes a surge of physical strength coursed through my body. Facing the beast, I became the Royal Werewolf Hunter. I screamed like a crazed banshee as I pushed the sharp iron head of the pole into the muscular chest, piercing the beating heart. One last enormous shove and the creature fell backwards, the tip of the make-shift spear impaling itself in the wooden floor beneath. The beast immediately began shifting back to its human form. A stranger's eyes stared blankly up at me. This was not the brother occupying Stan's persona.

***

I rushed to the back of the cottage where I found Neil lying among rotted blankets on a narrow bed. His hands were tied, and he was barely coherent from the blow to his head. He groaned when I tried to lift his shoulder. His head drooped onto his chest exposing a long gash through a bloody clump of hair.

"Shh. It's me, Laura. I have to get you out of here!"

The fear in my voice must have filtered through to him because he mumbled my name and sobbed. I lifted under his shoulder letting him rest against the headboard while I worked on the rope around his wrists. The rough binding badly chaffed his skin and there was blood on the fibers.

"Laura…it's really you. I thought…I was dreaming. My head is throbbing and…wait. I was making sandwiches. What happened to Stan? Is he alright?"

"Stan isn't Stan, but a shifter…a werewolf."

Neil blinked and opened his mouth, but I went on before he could question my sanity.

"Stan's persona was taken over after he was killed, and likely the man lying in the front room of this guest house is his brother and he assumed the body of a dog. These are the last of the Byrne brothers, the last werewolves from the pack the first Victor Darden hunted."

"But…they'd be centuries old!"

I had his hands freed.

"No time to explain, honey. Be quiet as we get out of here and back to the manor house. I have a job to finish."

Moving through the woods was slow going with Neil's arm draped over my shoulders. The side gate I used earlier came into view. I had an urge to take Neil inside and out of the chilly night. Staying focused, I moved us back several feet, keeping to the heavy shadows. I helped lower Neil to the ground where he could lean against the tree. A grimace tightened his mouth when his head touched the rough bark.

I quietly moved back to the edge of the woods.

The mansion had the look of a stone temple rising from a jungle of wild vegetation, washed in moonlight and awaiting a primitive religious ceremony. Something drew my gaze to the roof and the hideous gargoyles my ancestor had sent over from Ireland to complete his own monastery. And there he was. The werewolf stood on the mosey tiles, a hairy arm wrapped around the gargoyle. I hurried back to my husband.

"Neil," I whispered close to his ear. His eyelids fluttered partially open. I tried to keep the sharp edge of terror out of my voice.

"Listen carefully, honey. The second beast is on the roof, likely watching for us to reenter the mansion. I need to leave you here where you'll be safe until I can deal with him."

"No… you can't go alone," he said, struggling to get to his feet. It was obvious to both of us he'd be more of a hindrance than a help, as he slid back down against the trunk. A sheen of perspiration covered his forehead from the effort and pain.

"Stay here until I finish what my ancestors started. I'll be back love, promise.

I took off before I could change my mind. Weaving through the trees I made my way to the far corner of the mansion. The werewolf was still cozied-up to the gargoyle, both hideous monsters watching the woods for their prey. I reached the side gate grateful I'd left it open earlier. I watched the sky hoping for one of the wispy clouds that seemed to be chasing the full moon, to dull its light long enough for me to scoot down the path leading to the mud room door.

The werewolf that assumed Stan's identity was still searching the woods waiting for me to step out of the shadows. Suddenly, it looked up at the moon. throwing its huge hairy head back, howling like the devil himself.

As if he stirred the very heavens with that unholy sound, a cluster of gray clouds drifted past the bright yellow orb, throwing the grounds into sudden darkness. I scampered like a rabbit with a fox on its tail making the door just as the moon freed itself and drenched the ground in its obstinate glow. I knew the werewolf had sharp hearing, and before I made the door, I looked up as he moved out of sight.

He's heading inside.

DEATH STALKS DARDEN PLACE

My breath felt sharp in my chest, like I'd run a marathon. When I passed into the kitchen I walked directly to the sink. Opening the lower cabinet, I grabbed the small spray bottle I used for my plants. Pouring out the water I pulled the cork on a vial, filling the sprayer with the yellow potion. Not very intimidating as weapons go, but all I had. Well, not all. I pulled a long carving knife out of the butcher block on the counter. "That's better," I whispered, trying to give myself courage.

I moved from the kitchen to the hallway. I suspected the beast would check through the upstairs in case I hid among the many rooms while he was on the roof. I needed a safer place to carry out our killing game and the library sprang to mind. There was really no place to hide, but something drew me back there. I ran down the hallway, grateful the Persian carpet muffled the sound.

Like a woman under the influence of hypnosis, I crossed to the first bookcase. I had a wild thought. *There's a secret room built here.* I heard a thud from overhead. The beast was in our bedroom. I ran a hand near the middle of the shelving where the wood was thickest. Halfway down the case, I found it! A recessed latch blended completely into the dark wood. When I pulled it half the bookcase swung wide.

I gave a silent thanks to my great, great grandfather and stepping inside, pulled the shelf behind until I heard it click into place. It was as dark as a pit. I switched on my flashlight playing it over cobwebs and heavy threads of dust dangling from overhead beams. Holding an arm over my head to keep the tendrils out of my face, I moved deeper into the room. It was larger than I would have expected, when my knee hit against some furniture I stopped moving. My light shone off heavy wooden tables, pushed together forming a long workstation. Glass vials were suspended over soot-smudged burners. There were several glass plates inside a crumbling cardboard box along with an antique microscope.

A glass-fronted wooden case had five levels of shelves crowded with twenty glass jars. Each held an exotic plant, parts of animals that I couldn't identify, or types of spongy mushrooms, all suspended in amber liquid. "This was Victor's laboratory!" I murmured. A miasma of old chemicals and rotted specimens permeated the stagnant air.

I was moving deeper into the room when I heard a guttural sound from the other side of the false wall. I knew the hidden door latched behind me, but the smell of my presence would be strong. The werewolf would surely zero in on it. I had to see if Victor created other vials of the yellow liquid so I could be better prepared. I carelessly left the kitchen knife back in the library as I searched it. If

DEATH STALKS DARDEN PLACE

I could subdue the beast with the potion inside the sprayer, I'd have a chance to survive. I was all that stood between the creature and my injured husband.

The sound of books and furniture being thrown around the library hurried my movements as I lit up the wall at the back of the room. A tall walnut cabinet filled half the wall. It was filled with jars and vials suspended in metal cages.

This is it! I thought, as I opened the glass door, pulling out various colored liquids, looking for the yellow one with the black seeds. I'd nearly emptied the first two shelves when I saw the last vial cage pushed against the back. There were three full vials with the yellow, black speckled potion. Hoping the many years hadn't destroyed their potency, I put them in my pocket. Taking out the sprayer, I was wrapping my fingers on the door's pull latch when a scream from the other side echoed around the library in an avalanche of terror.

Neil! I knew the beast hadn't left the room, so Neil must have revived and come looking for me. The werewolf would either kill him or …turn him!

I couldn't let either happen, so gave the latch a hard jerk. Jumping back from the opening, I pressed myself against the wall praying the dark shadows that filled the room would blur my presence long enough for me to act.

A snort and low growl warned me the beast was moving toward the open doorway. I was completely vulnerable, but the sound of shoes scrapping the parquet floor stiffened my courage. A smell like bloody meat and wet wool began to swirl around me as the beast came closer.

He dropped his human burden with a grunt and entered the narrow opening. I held a vial and sprayer; intuition told me I needed to aim both at his face to be effective. *If he turns now…*

The beast looked left, his face turned away from me, and moved further into the room. I thought I'd lost my best chance. He was clearly hunting for me, but the heavy chemical odors in the lab must have confused his keen senses. I slid through the narrow opening, nearly tripping over the savaged body of the elderly family lawyer, Matthew Brimmer. I covered a relieved sob with my hand; it wasn't Neil! Brimmer must have stopped by on other legal matters and ran right into the monster.

I had an idea. I found the hidden lever to the door and pulled it up. The heavy door began to close, the faintest sound of a mechanism sounding like a trumpet blast. The werewolf spun around, seeing me standing in front of the closing doorway. Growling loudly, he tore across the room in time to shove an arm through the space left before the door locked into place. His face was hideous, and I smelled the rancid breath. It dawned on him; he had just trapped himself. He wouldn't take long to pull his arm free, destroying the door in the process.

My fingers were wrapped around the small sprayer. It began to heat up the closer I got to the beast. His face had to be covered with the potion, so he'd breathe in the droplets. He began to tear off the wood around the doorframe, stopping when I came closer to stare into his red eyes. *He knows me*, I thought.

Avoiding the huge grasping hand and arm, I brought the sprayer up, pressing the plunger until it was empty. I breathed in the acrid taste and odor of burning pelt and flesh. I uncorked another vial before the beast gave out a roar of recognition. I waited until he threw his head back in a deafening roar of pain, splashing the contents over his arm and chest.

The beast's agony was hellish. In less-than a minute his destruction was complete. He collapsed onto the floor, suspended by his arm until he returned to human form and his arm slipped free. I moved close enough to be certain he was dead. There were still small tuffs of black fur on Stan's cheeks, but these faded and disappeared as I watched. Streams of greasy smelling smoke rose in thin columns from his body, lost among the shadows of the secret room.

I had two vials left, pulled the cork on one and opened the door the rest of the way. Seeing the destruction of Stan's body, I was still hesitant.

With the door swung wide, the smell was nearly overpowering. I stepped to his head where gray smoke drifted from his ears, a silent scream pulling his mouth wide. I emptied the small vial down his throat, rushing back to the library before I was overcome with the strong fumes coming off the body. My fingers found the hidden lever and I watched as the door closed on the gruesome scene.

***

Neil was still leaning against the tree where I left him. I shook his shoulder gently, telling him it was time to go inside. His clothes were damp, and he shivered as I got my arm under him. As we moved toward the kitchen door he stopped.

"Laura. What's happened? I remember some kind of creature and Stan…Where's Stan? Is he…dead?"

"He was dead long before he came to Darden Place, Neil. I need to explain some Darden family history to you and show you a letter I received from my great-grandfather, Victor. But first, let's get you inside and cleaned up."

DEATH STALKS DARDEN PLACE

It had been four days since the Irish brothers turned life into a nightmare Poe would have appreciated. After a good night's rest, Neil was himself with no sign of concussion. We tried at normalcy with coffee and muffins and went into the library together. I wasn't sure what we'd find when I pulled the lever to open the door into the lab, but we had to know things were finished to feel safe again.

Neil now held the sprayer, refilled with the last of the potion, standing close to me as the door silently began to open. Sunlight streamed through the tall bay windows. Looking down, we saw a large grey pile of ash, stirring with small eddies of air released into the room. I looked up at Neil.

"I'll close it, honey, and it will never be opened again."

I turned away after pulling the lever and took Neil's hand. It felt hot and clammy to the touch. I looked back at him. He was rubbing his left arm. Worried, I pulled up the sleeve revealing deep puncture marks, the surrounding skin black with the poison injected into him.

"No!" I screamed as I dropped his arm, backing away.

Neil's breathing became rapid and harsh sounding. He rubbed his arm hard and groaned.

"Don't let it happen to me, Laura! Please!" he screamed in my frightened face.

Neil held the sprayer. We hadn't been in the library since that night and now I frantically looked around for the table where I left the kitchen knife. I knew what Neil was begging me to do, but I didn't know if I could find the courage to do it. The long butcher knife glinted in the sunlight falling across a tall reading table near the windows.

I looked back at Neil, doubled over in pain. The sounds of cracking and popping signaled the beginning of the shift from my loving husband into savage werewolf. Resolutely gripping the knife, I ran back to where he lay writhing with the pain of legs and arms torn from sockets while bones elongated into distorted non-human shapes. In a few seconds it would be complete, and Neil would have become a grotesque monster and I'd be dead.

I took a deep breath, shouting, "I'll love you forever!" just before plunging the knife up to its hilt through his exposed chest.

I stood frozen over his body, watching as it morphed back into fully human…fully Neil. Fully dead.

***

This was the end of my responsibility as the last of the Royal Werewolf Hunters. In fact, I was the very last of the long line of Dardens. I studied my husband's still form. The cold touch of death leached the color from his face, leaving him a sleeping marble statue. I couldn't break down. Not yet.

I walked out of the library, the stench of death in my nostrils. Moving up the circular stairs like a sleepwalker, I entered our bedroom and pulled a large suitcase from the closet. There would eventually be an investigation into the old lawyer's disappearance. The town Sheriff had introduced himself to us when we first arrived at Darden Place, so our presence was established. I couldn't answer questions about the death of the two men lying in the library, or they'd lock me in a prison for the criminally insane.

My decision was instant. I would return to my family's roots. Throwing what I could into the suitcase, I pulled out my phone and called Iberian Air to book a one-way flight to Ireland. I left a note on the kitchen table.

"I fought them with all my strength, but it wasn't enough to save Neil or Mr. Bremmer. I will not live with the guilt of knowing in the end, the monsters won."

THE CORNER LOT

Shawn D Brink

Amos was almost 10 years old the day he strolled down the sidewalk with a well-loved baseball in his grip. That ball was a birthday present from his father, given only months before his dad left for the war.

He walked along the corner lot that existed about a block from his home. He used to avoid that lot because of the weird vibes it put out. But these days, Amos wanted those vibes because they dulled the pain created by his dad's absence.

The lot sat on the edge of town, adjacent to a cornfield. Amos stared at the field for a moment. The corn stood tall, swaying with the breeze like waves on water.

There was an old house on that lot, but Amos could only see the second story. A tall, wooden privacy fence, higher than Amos' head, ran along the edge of the sidewalk, blocking the lower half of the house from view.

From what he could see, the house was in ruins. The paint was pealing. The glass in many of the windows was spiderwebbed with cracks. Vines crept up the house's exterior siding, wrapping around the downspouts and window frames, as if nature itself was slowly pulling the house back to the dirt from which it came.

He rounded the property's corner, and there stood the three Sullivan brothers, the youngest being a full year older than Amos. They were preoccupied with trying to kill a mouse they'd cornered against the fence.

Amos turned around, hoping for a quick retreat, praying those bullies hadn't noticed his presence. In his haste, he tripped over his own feet and fell to the ground. He landed face down. When he rolled over, the Sullivans surrounded him. Out of the corner of his eye, he saw the mouse scurry across the street and into the cornfield.

"Well, lookie here," the biggest sneered as he yanked Amos to his feet. "I do believe we've found a lost little baby!"

"I—I—I—I'm not a b—b—b—baby." Amos stuttered. This was something he always did when frightened.

"Babies shouldn't have grown-up toys," the bully bellowed as he wrenched the ball away.

"N–No! Th–Th–Th–That's my d–d–dad's!"

"Really?" the big Sullivan chuckled. "Well, it looks crappy. Don't your dad take care of his stuff?"

The Sullivans began to laugh, and Amos felt very small. He wanted to tell them that the ball had been new when his dad gave it to him. He wanted to tell them how important that ball was. He wanted to tell them off. In the end, he said nothing.

"Do you want it back?"

Amos nodded vigorously.

"Here you go." He presented the ball to Amos. "Take it."

Amos lunged for it, but the bully was faster and tossed it over the fence. "Oops, you'd better go after it."

Before Amos could even think of what to do, the Sullivans picked him up and hoisted him over the top of the fence.

He landed head-first. His ears rang as he staggered to his feet.

On this side of the fence, those strange vibes were stronger. They came to him like whispers rising from the soil – incoherent, indecipherable whispers that made Amos squirm.

He pressed his back against the fence, staring at a yard as neglected as the house. Grass grew tall here, almost as tall as himself. Among the grass, thistles angled their purple blooms his direction, like monstrous eyes. Also, saplings bordering on treehood cast unnaturally dark shadows.

Amos flinched. Something touched his foot. He looked down.

It was his ball. Had it been there the whole time, or had it been rolled to him?

"If that's your ball, then take it."

"W—w—who's there?" Amos stammered.

"My gosh, boy, you sound more like an owl than a child. You are a child, aren't you?"

Amos nodded. He stared hard, searching for the owner of that tenor voice, but foliage hid the lurker.

"What's your name?"

"A—A—Amos," he stammered.

The grass parted. A figure emerged. "Well, Amos, it's nice to meet you."

The man was short for an adult, about Amos' height. He was thin as a beanpole and wore no shirt or shoes, just a pair of faded denim overalls. Much of his face was hidden behind long and unruly graying hair, beard, and mustache.

But what captivated Amos most were his eyes. The iris' appeared dark, almost black. They sparkled like polished onyx.

"How did you end up here on this side of the fence?" the man asked.

Amos shrugged. Shame held his tongue.

"Did the Sullivans do this to you?"

Amos shrugged again.

"I'm not going to hurt ya." The man's overgrown mustache hairs fluttered as he spoke. "I just want to know what happened to you."

THE CORNER LOT

"The S–S–Sullivans were p–picking on me," he managed to say. "Then, th–they th–th–th–threw me over the f–f–fence."

"Sullivans!" the man scoffed. "They're all rotten. Why, when I was a boy, their daddy and his brothers did the same to me. I guess the apple don't fall far from the tree, am I right?"

Amos wasn't sure if he was expected to answer. So, he remained silent, which must have been okay because the stranger continued talking.

"The house was newer back then – back when they used to bully me. The fence was stronger too, not a single loose board anywhere."

"H–Have you been here a l–l–long t–t–time?" Amos asked.

The man nodded slowly.

"All a–a–alone?"

The man's black eyes shimmered in the dim light. After a moment that felt longer than it probably was, he spoke. "Alone? No, I was never alone. This lot kept me company."

"Th—Th—This l–l–lot?"

"Yes," he answered. "This property can feed you. It can keep you company when you are feeling lonely. It can console you and let you know everything's okay, even when it's not." The man grinned a cold grin. "Be still for a moment. I bet you'll hear it calling you. Just listen."

Amos recalled those vibes and how strong they felt when he'd first been thrown over the fence. He listened now and those whispers came to him once more. They came to him from under his feet, rising from the ground itself. They were stronger than before – seductive whispers, enticing whispers. Unlike earlier, he could understand what they were saying. '*Stay here and be safe with us,*' they said.

Part of him wanted that. He missed his father so much. He missed the safety of being part of a complete family – of having somebody stick up for him and protect him from bullies like the Sullivans.

'*We can be your family,*' the lot whispered. '*If you stay.*'

He shook his head. He couldn't leave his mother. She missed his dad too. If he left, then she'd really be alone.

The man's rising voice brought Amos from his trance. "The lot changes you! It hardens you, makes you strong! It provides for you and takes care of you as if you were its own kin!"

'*It's true. We can make you strong. We'll be your family. Let us change you.*'

"N–No, my m–mother needs me," Amos answered.

The man drew nearer. Amos could see those eyes in perfect clarity. They held a darkness, but also sympathy. "You still haven't picked up your ball."

Amos slid down the fence, feeling its roughness through his shirt and against his spine as he skidded along. He grabbed the ball and rose back up. It felt good to hold it. He felt his father's love in its ragged stitching, and remembered hours spent playing catch with him before he left.

"You don't belong here," the man gestured toward the fence. "You need to be out there. You need to be waiting with your mother for your father's return. How long has your dad been at war?"

"Ab–About a y–year." Had he told this man about how the war stole his father away?

The grass, thistles, and saplings swayed as if caught in a breeze. But Amos felt no breeze.

The man's voice grew deeper – darker. "A boy needs his freedom. A boy needs his family."

The foliage stopped mid-sway. All was still. In the silence, Amos stared deeply into those onyx-eyes and a chill escaped him.

The man pointed toward the fence. "These two fence boards are loose. When I pull them off, I want you to stay put until all the commotion is over. Then wait for my command."

Amos didn't respond.

"Do you understand me? It's crucial that you understand. Do not come out until I say. If you come out early, I can't guarantee your safety."

Amos nodded.

In one fluid movement, the man slid up to the fence. With a pop, one of the boards came loose and fell to the ground. A second closely followed.

The Sullivan boys were still there. "Lookie," Amos heard one of them say. "The baby is trying to get out of his playpen."

The man stood in the gap, bathed in the comparatively bright light that passed through from the far side of the fence. He turned his head back toward Amos for just a moment, a black silhouette superimposed on a white backdrop. "Those Sullivans won't be bothering you no more."

Amos trembled at the sight. The man's once-black eyes now flamed crimson, and all that hair bristled like the back of a wild dog just before it attacks.

The creature blinked those awful eyes once. Then, it vanished through the opening.

Amos closed his eyes and covered his ears, but it wasn't enough to block out the screams coming from the opposite side of the fence – bloodcurdling screams.

After a while, the screams stopped. He uncovered his ears and opened his eyes.

THE CORNER LOT

All the grass angled toward him, and the thistles watched intently from under the saplings' shade. Whispers bubbled up from the ground beneath, clearer than ever. *'You could still stay. You could be our son. We would love you and take good care of you.'*

Amos felt the grass caress his ankles as the purple-eyed thistles leaned in further. Above his head, the saplings bent low.

For a moment, he considered the lot's proposal. But then, he thought of his mother and how sad she'd be if he didn't come home. "No. Mom needs me more than you do." His stutter was gone, as was his fear.

Something large flew over the fence and landed near him. It was the youngest Sullivan. "Are you okay?" Amos asked.

The kid didn't respond. His face was unnaturally pale with a frozen expression of sheer terror. He laid in the fetal position. One of his feet was missing a shoe. The toes on that foot twitched minutely. Other than that, he remained still as stone.

The young Sullivan moaned as the surrounding foliage leaned in, growing closer, and then closer still. He began to tremble as the grass slid up his shirt and out the top of his collar, braiding their thin strands into his hair.

A voice came from the far side of the fence. "One can leave the corner lot when replaced by another." The voice was like that of the onyx-eyed man, but wilder – stronger. "If you wish to leave, you may do so now."

'You may go, but it's not required. We're quite fond of you. You may stay if you wish.'

"I can't," Amos answered as he dared peek through the opening in the fence. The sun hid behind dark rainclouds, yet it was brighter here than within the boundaries of the fence.

He stepped through. The onyx-eyed man and the two older Sullivans were nowhere to be seen. Something that could have been blood puddled the sidewalk. Other than that, the space was vacant except for a single shoe, which sat nearby, leaning against the fence.

He looked toward the cornfield, wondering what horrific acts those stalks had observed, knowing they were likely the sole witnesses, and wouldn't tell a soul.

Rain started and almost instantly became a downpour. Within a minute, the blood (Amos was positive that's what it was) washed away down the street, and everything smelled fresh – renewed.

He turned back toward the opening in the fence, but it was gone. In its place were two new boards. He pressed against them, wondering if they were real. They were.

He walked the perimeter of the lot and noticed for the first time, no gate existed, just an unending fence.

He knew he'd come full circle when he spied that abandoned shoe leaning against the fence. He stood still beside that shoe and listened hard, but the lot no longer whispered to him.

With a shrug, he picked up the shoe and chucked it over the fence. Then, with ball in hand, he walked home where he knew his mother would be waiting.

And maybe his father too.

THE NIGHTMARE GAME

Janet Post

"Where did you find it?" Hillary asked.

"It was in front of Old Lady Crapapple's house. I was walking by and there it was, laying on the bottom step."

Hillary turned the ancient gaming system over in her hands several times. "Were there any controllers?"

Kushal Kumaran shot her a side eye. "I didn't think to look. It seems in good condition and there's a game inserted into the player."

"Let's walk back and check."

The two of them trotted down Cedar Street in their small town of Mt. Vernon, Washington. They lived in the old part of town. The houses had been built in the twenties or earlier. Tall three-story wood structures with old shingle roofs, bow windows, towers, and steep steps leading up to the sagging front porches. Some had been renovated and painted shiny blue, cream, and yellow, but many wore ancient coats of peeling paint like houses with psoriasis, gray siding showing through. All had at least two brick chimneys.

Mrs. Crabapple, AKA Old Lady Crapapple, had never liked children. Her house was in probably the worst condition of any house on the block. Black smoke shot in plumes out of the chimney in the middle of the house. The steps leading up the embankment to her dilapidated porch were cracked concrete. One had collapsed completely.

Hillary glanced up at the house. "She's watching us. This is some kind of trap."

Kushal shook his head. "No, no, I believe she threw it out. Why would she try to trap us?"

"Look, the curtain moved."

"You are not thinking straightly." Kushal reached into a crevasse under the collapsed stair and pulled out a controller. He held it up triumphantly. "Perhaps we should take this to Angel. He can play games on anything. It's all he does every day."

"He's in a wheelchair," Hillary said. "It's good he's good at something he can do inside. Really good."

Kushal stopped. "But, maybe you are correct in assuming this is a trap. Perhaps, we should throw it into the nearest waste disposal container. We are tempting the fates by trying to play on this old system."

Hillary rolled her eyes. "You own a video game system?"

"Uh, no."

"Well neither do I. It would be neat to have one we could play on."

"I feel sure my mother would not approve and neither would Father Frank or Father Martin."

"You're too obsessed with your religion, Kushal. Be happy. Forget the good Catholic boy stuff for a freaking minute and have some fun."

Kushal sighed. "When you put it that way, I feel incredibly stupid."

Angel Dodson lived two blocks over on River Street in a one-floor ranch-style house equipped with a ramp to get from the sidewalk to the house, and a wide entrance.

Hillary knocked. It was three in the afternoon. Angel's mother had died in the car accident that crippled him and his dad had to work two jobs to pay all the bills. No one answered so Hillary yelled. "Angel, open up. It's Hillary and Kushal."

The door clicked and swung open. There were lots of automated gizmos in Angel's house to help him get around and use the appliances and the facilities he needed. Hillary walked in followed closely by Kushal. "Where are you, my friend?" Kushal called.

The house had little furniture, leaving wide avenues for Angel's chair. "I be chillin' in my room," Angel yelled from the depths of the house.

Hillary and Kushal knew the way. Angel was parked in front of his desk. An open Mac Book Pro sat on it. Angel was not playing games.

"You lurk on the dark web?" Hillary asked. The page open on the laptop had ads for life-like, anatomically correct dolls.

Angel didn't seem at all embarrassed. "You think a dude like me gonna get a real woman? I don't think so. I'm saving up for this one." He pointed to a red-headed doll, mostly naked. "She does all kinds of cool stuff."

Hillary slammed the laptop closed. "I don't ever want to see that again."

"Why you here, anyway?" Angel asked. He whirled his electric chair around and faced them.

"We found this," Kushal said as he produced the video game.

Angel took the game and examined it. "This game old. Real old. Like 1980s old. The CD-i dates to the 1980s when gaming companies were trying to find a way to jump from cartridge games to compact discs. Never took off. Not many were even sold. Like a hundred or something."

"We have a controller," Kushal said. He handed it to Angel. "Can you make it work? It has a CD in it."

Angel plugged it in. Lights blinked and the TV on Angel's dresser lit up. "What the hell?" Angel said. "It ain't even connected. A Ouija board

THE NIGHTMARE GAME

popped up on the screen with a little heart-shaped disc floating around and around. Instead of letters and numbers, the board had faces with names under them. Real ugly, spooky, creepy faces. Smoke or fog drifted across the screen.

Kushal backed away. "This is sinful. We should not be looking at it." Kushal's family may have come from India, but they were devout Catholics. Kushal went to church twice a week. "This is demonic." He made the sign of the cross, pulled a silver cross out from under his shirt and kissed it.

"Choose your form." A deep voice emanated from all around them. Not from the TV but hanging in the air like a cloud of sound.

"I am not going to participate in this highly heretical game," Kushal announced and turned to go. They were in Angel's room. When Kushal went to leave, he screamed. "Where is the door?"

Hillary spun, staring at all four bedroom walls. Where posters and photos used to hang, only black walls existed. Colors shifted across the black like iridescent gems. It wasn't pretty, it was terrifying.

"Choose your form."

"Pick an avatar," Angel yelled. "Hurry."

The walls were slowly closing in on them. "Anything but the Evilla witch," Angel hissed. "Anything but her. I can tell she bad."

Hillary put her finger on the heart-shaped counter. The board with the faces now floated in front of them. She dragged it toward Cara Blank, pictured as a tall woman kind of like Morticia Adams only under her long black hair her face was a blank white oval.

Hillary appeared to fight with the counter. It kept moving up, toward the witch, Evilla, while Hillary tried to push it to Cara. She finally won the fight. As soon as the counter was on Cara Blank, Hillary disappeared.

Kushal shrieked and fell against the black shimmering wall now only a foot away. He and Angel were being boxed in. Only they and the board remained in the room. "Pick one," Angel said. "Or we gonna die." Angel dragged the counter using both hands to the one reading Axel Blade. The character was black, wore dread locks, an over-sized T-shirt, and baggy pants. "This has got to be me."

As soon as the counter was on the icon, Angel was gone, his chair empty.

Kushal, hyperventilating, thought about his parents, his church, the sanctuary, Father Frank, comfortable and fat. His head swam and sweat dripped from his black hair down his brown face. The wall behind touched him. He screamed, stuck his fingers on the counter and moved it to Professor Bonamy Stogumber. How could a professor be a bad person? The face of the avatar cleared for a minute and returned as a heavy-set middled-aged man with thick reddish hair and pink cheeks.

OMG a white guy. As soon as the counter touched the icon, Kushal felt his brains scramble, his limbs felt light, and he watched in horror as his legs and torso disappeared.

Then everything went black.

Hillary's eyes opened. The first thing she noticed was the stench and wetness. She lay in some stinking slop that smelled like dead fish. It was so dark she couldn't see her own hand. She patted all around her and felt something. She pulled it up and quickly realized it was a skeletonized hand. The fingers and wrist bones were evident. She tried to scream but couldn't. Then she remembered the avatar for Cara Blank. It had no face. Did she now have no face? She scrambled to her knees, wiped her hands on her dress, and felt her face. If she could have screamed, she would have. She had no mouth, no nose, no eyes.

Glimmers of light appeared behind her. She felt in her hair, drew some of the lank tresses aside and viewed her new world. It was dark out, but a full moon turned the world an eerie blue. Her eyes were on the back of her head. She felt around in her hair and found her nose. Her mouth was there but big stiches had closed it shut.

She swiveled her head around to see where she was. A stone sat a foot away. A headstone. She was in a graveyard and currently standing in a grave. Parts of the dead person's body floated in the muck which reached her knees.

Gagging behind her sewn-shut lips she leapt out of the muck. A mound of dirt, more headstones, and a statue of a griffin surrounded her. When she looked beyond them, she saw a black iron fence with spikes. A bolt of lightning shot across the moon followed by a crack of thunder and a body splatted into the grave she'd landed in. It had to be Angel. She'd watched movies that started with an evil game, a hundred times. Had to be Angel or Kushal.

A groan erupted followed by coughing. "I'm Angel." He sat up and spit out the foul dirt. "Where we at?"

"Graveyard," Hillary said in a muffled voice which made it sound like rrravmmard.

"What?"

She pointed to a body part floating beside Angel. She parted her hair more and looked Angel over. He was a black man, looked in his twenties, with long dread locks, wearing a filthy T-shirt.

"Jeez, Hillary, where's yer fricking face?"

THE NIGHTMARE GAME

She turned around and showed him by pulling her hair aside. "It's on backwards. What in all that's holy? And your mouth is stitched shut." He picked at the string holding her lips closed and found a loose end. In a minute, he'd pulled it all off and Hillary could talk.

"Thank you," she said. "Thank you so much."

"Your entire face is still on the back of your head which just ain't right."

Another bolt of lightning followed by thunder and a large man with red hair landed on top of Ange, I knocking him back into the sludge of the grave. Hillary shoved the big guy, who had to be Kushal, off Angel. Angel slowly rose from the muck, his face dripping. He rolled onto his back. "Well, that sucked."

When Angel smiled, Hillary gasped. "You have fangs, Angel. You're a vampire."

"What happened?" Kushal asked. "Where am I?" He lay on his back in the wet grass breathing like every breath was going to be his last. His round belly rose and fell. "Where am I?" He glanced at Hillary and then over at Kushal. "Who in heck are you?"

Hillary poked him with the pointy toe of her black high heel. "I'm Hillary."

"You do not have a face which I am sorry to say is very frightening."

Hillary turned around and pulled her hair aside. "Oh, my Jesus," Kushal said.

"Tell me about it."

"If that is Hillary," he pointed at Angel, "then you must be . . ."

"Yeah, I'm Angel. Where the hell are we? Did we get sucked into a demonic world? That can't be real."

"Mybe Old Lady Crapapple is a real witch and cursed the game, Hillary said. "She hates kids. She probably did this to us on purpose."

Angel pulled himself to his feet using the tombstone. He rubbed some dirt off and read. "Here lies Angel Dodson. A legless twerp to the end. 2009-2023."

Angel leaped back tripping over Kushal and falling into the mucky grave. "It's gotta be Old Lady Crapapple," Hillary said.

***

They sat on a tomb attempting to pull themselves together. All were scared witless. There was a tombstone for each of them in the graveyard. "What are we supposed to do now?" Kushal asked. His head was bent so low his long red hair touched his chubby knees.

THE NIGHTMARE GAME

"Well, in the movie, this is where the non-player comes in and gives the players direction. Remember the guy who drove the Land Rover?"

Hillary was sitting sideways so she could see. "I don't see anyone. Do you?" She would have rolled her eyes, but with them hidden by her hair it was a wasted effort.

A blob appeared, crossing the face of the full moon. "What's that?" Angel said.

The blob flew erratically, up and down, wobbling, dropping close to the ground, then soaring. When they could finally see, Hillary burst out. "It's a freaking fat fairy. A fat fairy dressed in black with black wings. She's so overweight, she can barely fly."

The fairy landed in front of them, flopped onto her face, and then lifted her head. A donut hung out of her mouth. There was a litter of crumbs across the front of her black sparkly dress. Her wings folded back, and she sat up. "Let me finish this," she said as she chewed and swallowed. "Chocolate cream. My favorite."

"Oh my god," Hillary said.

"What? I was hungry."

"Never mind, if you please," Kushal said as he pushed long red hair out of his face. "Do you have a message for us?"

The fairy's eyes opened wide. She had blond hair and reminded Hillary of someone she knew.

"Right," the fairy said as she pulled a crumpled piece of paper out of the front of her dress. "I am Ariel Buttertub. Your mission, if you choose to accept it."

"Mission impossible," Angel whispered into Hillary's hair. "It's like we're caught in a bad movie."

"If you please," Ariel stood up and stated in an imposing voice. "You must kill the witch Evilla before she sucks all your souls out of your bodies. To do this, you must find her. She lives there." Ariel pointed through the mist to an imposing hill with a massive building on its top. "Be aware, she lives off the souls of children so she will be after the three of you like white on rice."

"Are there any other children here?" Hillary asked. "And where are we?"

Ariel chuckled, a sound like a string of burps. "No, my children. You are the only ones."

"How do we kill her?" Kushal asked.

Ariel pointed at him. "First you must stalk and destroy Slenderman."

All three kids gasped as one. "No!" Kushal said. "He is the evilest one. He is too terrifying. We will surely die."

Practical as always, Hillary asked. "So, what's Slenderman got we need to kill Evilla?"

THE NIGHTMARE GAME

"He possesses the Talisman Ring. When you have it, you will be able to enter Evilla's castle and kill her."

Ariel's wings fluttered. "I must be gone. Steak and French fries await."

"No wait," Angel jumped up and grabbed Ariel's left wing. "How do you kill the witch? And you didn't tell us where we are."

"You are in the land of your nightmares. Whatever you fear, is what you will face. You have fabricated this world out of your own bad dreams and fears. To escape, you must overcome them all."

Angel hung on. "What kills Evilla?"

Ariel laughed. "Puppies, flowers, good deeds, and kind thoughts. All of these things and more will suck the evil out of her and drain her dry. She feeds on fear. She will try to hurt you and suck off your pain. You must think happy thoughts no matter what she does. Sing. Sing happy songs. All of the happiest songs you can think of."

"I can't sing," Kushal said. "I sound like someone is slaughtering a cat."

"Me either," Hillary said. "I tried out for choir. They laughed at me and made me leave. I like to sing. I'm just bad at it. What about you Angel?"

Angel shook his head. "I can carry a tune, but I don't know any songs."

"I'm out of here," Ariel said. "Kill Evilla or you will never leave the Nightmare Game." Ariel threw off Angel's hand and lumbered along between tombstones picking up speed, when she was running fast enough, she launched herself into the air and flew away.

Hillary sat on the tomb. "Wonderful. Now what do we do?"

A black cat meandered into the graveyard and approached them. It rubbed against Hillary's legs, and she absently reached down and stroked it. It meowed.

"What?" Kushal said. "I didn't quite understand you."

The cat meowed, squalled, and screeched. "Oh," Kushal said. "The cat knows how to get to Slenderman. He wishes us to follow, though I am quite sure I never want to see Slenderman. Certainly not here."

"You can speak to animals?" Angel asked.

Kushal looked thoughtful, an incongruous expression on his chubby red face. "I believe I can. I wonder why."

"We all have strengths. In the movie they were accessed by pressing your left shoulder." He pushed his shoulder a bunch of times and nothing happened.

"They're here," Hillary said. She'd pulled her dress up and was examining her butt. "I can watch my own back. That's one of my strengths. I can cast spells if I have my spell book. Great, I wonder where that is. I have one more strength but it's under my left cheek and I can't read it."

"I'll look." Angel leaped off the tomb to catch a glimpse of her rear end.

"No, you don't, perv. It will have to remain a mystery."

Kushal had stepped behind the tomb and dropped his brown corduroy pants. "I can speak any language. I have a man purse somewhere around here full of necessary stuff." He grunted and bent down further. "Looks like I'm strong, too. And, uh, my farts can be deadly. Slenderman is particularly susceptible." He turned his head to look at Hillary. "Weaknesses are on the other cheek. "Says I'm slow, which I figured, afraid of just about everything, and prone to flatulence."

"Oh, God, you fart, and your farts are deadly?"

"Well, it's not my fault. This is just an avatar. I can't help it if it gets gas. What are your weaknesses, Hillary?"

"I'm a bitch."

Kushal and Angel broke out in loud laughter.

"My vision is limited, which is obvious, my dress limits movement, and I'm terrified of Slenderman."

Kushal and Hillary concentrated their attention on Angel. "Well?"

"I looked. My strengths are pretty good. I'm a vampire so I'm immortal. I'm also very strong and can fly. I can hypnotize creatures and humans. My weaknesses are I need to feed on blood frequently." He stopped and his eyes turned red as he looked at them. They both backed up a foot. "Holy water is deadly, and flatulence can make me sick."

Kushal burst out laughing. "So, if you're near me when I fart, you get sick."

"I don't count it as a weakness," Angel said. "It would make me sick anyway. I have one more strength. I'm fearless."

The cat meowed. "It wants us to follow him," Kushal said. More meowing. "His name is George." Kushal closed his eyes and farted. Angel leapt away in a huge bound that took him out of the cemetery. "Sorry," Kushal called.

***

Rain began with a dribble then turned into a deluge. Hillary wanted to pull the hood of her cloak over her head but then she'd be blind, so the rain drenched her head, hair, and non-face face. Kushal's red hair hung in clumps around his round features, and Angel pulled his hood over his head and huddled inside of it. He was laughing. "Look, Hill." He yelled in glee and did a dance. I can walk. He ran a few steps and took off flying, circled them, and landed next to Hillary. "This is great," he said. "I haven't been able to walk since the accident."

Angel's mother had been driving drunk when she crashed into a forest, killed herself, and crippled Angel. His father had to work two jobs to care for him and keep their medical insurance, so he was alone in his chair a lot. His father made him feel like a burden, like it was his fault he couldn't walk and needed care, like it was his fault his dad had to work two jobs. A nurse came in once a day to check on him and the medical insurance only covered a small portion of the cost for the nurse.

"I guess this is kind of cool for you. Being able to walk after sitting in that chair for three years."

"You have no idea. And I can even fly." He took off flying over them, then higher as the cat led them down a gravel road barely visible in the dark and heavy rain. "I'll fly ahead and see if I can tell where we're going."

They followed the cat into a dark forest. The trees appeared menacing, their limbs grabbing Hillary's hair and her dress and tearing at them. Kushal moaned and groaned. "I've never been fat. Why must I be now? I do not understand where we are or what is happening."

Angel swooped down. "We're stuck in a video game, dude. I already told you."

"But how can this be? It is not possible."

"It's Halloween eve," Hillary said. "The spirits can pass into the real world. Anything is possible. And Old Lady Crapapple probably cursed that game console, and we picked it up like the stupid kids we are, and now we're stuck in a game. We've all seen these kinds of movies. We shoulda known better."

Angel landed next to Hillary. "Can't fly. The trees are too thick."

"Did you see where we're going?"

"There's a creepy old house on the other side of the woods. Probably where Slenderman lives."

Hillary sobbed and shook with fear. "Like I wasn't scared enough already. I hate Slenderman."

Angel patted her shoulder. "You know, you kind of look like him from the front. No face, tall and skinny. Except you're wearing a dress. Maybe he'll like you." He lifted his eyebrows twice in a row and grinned salaciously. "You know as in liked liked."

Hillary moaned. "No, no, no. Slenderman hitting on me? I'd die."

"That reminds me. Did you get a look at your other strength?"

"No, it's under my right ass cheek. I can't see it."

"We need to know what it is. Just give me a peek. It'll only take a minute and it's not like this is your real body. It's Cara Blank, not Hillary. Lemme look."

"Angel, I'm partially blind from the hair and the rain, and grumpy. Now is not the time."

"But we may need to know."

"Allow him to see," Kushal said. "We can shelter in that cave over there and get out of the rain."

"Oh, for pity's sake," Hillary grumbled. When they headed for the cave, the cat howled and hissed.

"Maybe we should listen to the cat," Angel said. "Kushal, what's it saying?"

"Do not go into the cave, it's more dangerous than Slenderman."

"I'm sopping wet," Hillary said in a sharp voice. "It can't hurt to just stand where it's dry for five freaking minutes."

The cat launched itself at Kushal and clung to his leg howling. "George says don't do it."

Hillary waved him off and stepped into the shelter of the cave's opening. "This is great. No rain." She used the bottom of her dress to wipe the water off her hair and clear her eyes. Angel stepped beside her and stopped. "I hear something."

"You have super hearing," Hillary said. "It's probably so deep inside the cave we'll never see it. Just one more minute. Kushal, can you make George shut up?"

The cat was screeching.

Something huge hit Hillary in her non face. She felt fangs sink into it and heard a loud slurping.

"Vampire bats!" Kushal screeched as one landed on his chest and sank its inch-long fangs into his neck. Angel ripped it off as more bats erupted from the depths of the cave. "Run!" Angel yelled as he ran around, ripping the one off Hillary and waving the rest away. "Shoo! Go away. Scram," he shouted. "I am your leader. Leave these people alone."

The bats hovered over their heads in a frustrated flock as they ran through the woods following George who raced down narrow paths through thick underbrush and brambles. Angel kept the bats off them as they ducked low to get through the bushes. Hillary had a hard time trying to crawl backwards. She finally hooked her fingers in Kushal's belt and allowed him to lead her. Then he farted a green cloud of gas and Hillary passed out. Angel's white face was yellow as he lifted Hillary by her dress and carried her after Kushal.

"Dude." Angel gagged. "Don't ever do that again.

"I can't help it. It's one of my strengths and weaknesses all in one. They come on, my stomach fills, and then I just let it rip. Sorry."

"Can you make it happen?"

"I don't know. I'm kind of afraid to try. You know. Sharts."

They popped out of the brambles, Kushal and Hillary sporting scratches and bleeding cuts. Angel shuddered and slowly licked a long scratch on Hillary's arm. She came to and screamed. "Stop it."

Angel crumpled into a ball of misery. "I'm so sorry. I'm starving."

"You can eat Slenderman with my blessing."

When the underbrush finally came to an end, they stopped. "I can't," Hillary said. "Just look at them. All staring right at us."

The path to Slenderman's old mansion was lined with antique dolls with ceramic heads. Some had solid bodies, some of the bodies were in pieces. There had to be a hundred of them and all of their glass eyes were focused on the three of them. As Hillary watched, one blinked. "Oh crap, they're alive," she said.

"If we want out of this nightmare, we have to get the Talisman Ring. It's in there, Hillary," Angel said. "We have to go down the pathway."

"Why dolls? It's like a hundred Chuckies. I hated Child's Play movies. All of them."

"Come with me," Kushal said and held out his hand. "I am not afraid. I've never seen Child's Play. My parents don't allow me to watch horror movies, so a lot of old dolls mean nothing to me."

"If you don't mind," Angel said. "I'm gonna fly over all of them, scope out the house from the air, see what's going on."

Kushal waved him on. "Good plan. I'll lead Hillary through the dolls."

"Make sure you get to the house," Angel said. "Your gas is our best and only weapon. If you got anything to eat in that bag you're carrying it, eat it now."

Kushal opened the satchel and looked inside. "Bean burritos. My favorite."

Hillary smiled. "If they don't give you gas, nothing will."

Kushal scarfed up two burritos as Angel took off flying high over Slenderman's house. When Kushal had eaten the burritos, he took Hillary's hand. She quickly removed it from his grip and wiped it off on her dress. "Geez, get rid of the grease."

THE NIGHTMARE GAME

"Sorry." Kushal wiped his hands off on his corduroy pants. "Ready?"

"No, but since I can't see where I'm going, it doesn't matter that much. And as I pass, all I'll see is the back of their heads."

However, when they'd gone three feet down the winding pathway through the dolls, Hillary screamed. "Oh my god, they're turning their heads and watching us."

"Close your eyes, Hill. Don't look at them."

Hillary screamed again. "Slenderman. He's here."

Kushal whirled around. Slenderman had appeared behind them, following slowly, his hands were tentacles reaching for Hillary. "Run," Kushal said and yanked Hillary after him. She stumbled and fell on one of the dolls. Its eyes were inches from hers. She screamed again, scrambled to her feet, fueled by terror, and ran blindly after Kushal.

Angel suddenly swooped down and attacked Slenderman, wrapped his arms around Slenderman's body, and sank his teeth in the white neck above the collar of his shirt and tie.

While this was going on, Kushal and Hillary reached the porch. Hillary sank down on the concrete steps panting, her face covered by hair. She pushed it aside and saw Kushal staring past her at the doll-lined path, Angel and Slenderman. "Is he eating him?" Hillary asked.

"Don't look. Slenderman just wrapped his tentacles around Angel and tossed him into the woods. He's coming down the path toward us."

Hillary jumped up, turned around, and backed against the wall of the old mansion. "He's coming for us," she said. "Do something, Kushal. You ate the damn burritos. Fart!"

"I don't feel any gas in my stomach," he moaned. "I don't think I can."

"It's your superpower, your strength. Try."

Kushal turned his butt and pointed it at Slenderman who was stalking slowly toward them.

"Fart," Hillary said.

"I gotta wait until he's closer."

"Oh, God, we're gonna die," she wailed. Slenderman wore a black suit, was tall and thin. He had a white shirt and a black tie under the suit coat. His face was blank. No features at all. Where fingers and hands should have been long tentacles reached toward them. Angel rose from the trees and flew at Slenderman. He dive bombed him. Slenderman was momentarily distracted.

"I think I feel one coming on," Kushal said.

"Hold it. Wait another minute until he's closer," Hillary said in a whisper. She spotted the

THE NIGHTMARE GAME

Talisman Ring hanging on a chain around Slenderman's neck. Angel flew higher and Slenderman started running for Hillary and Kushal. "Now," Hillary whispered. "Do it."

Kushal's face contorted and he lifted one leg slightly. The sound of the fart seemed enormous as Kushal ripped off a huge ball of noxious gas. It was green and hit Slenderman right in his featureless face.

Slenderman stumbled, wobbled, tripped over some of the dolls scattering their hideous little heads. He dropped to his knees and Kushal backed toward him. "I can feel another one coming on."

"Let him have it." Angel's voice came from above the house.

Kushal's screwed up his face as he concentrated. "I think it's gonna be a big one." He backed toward Slenderman who was crawling through tall grass but obviously failing. Kushal passed Slenderman and sat on his nonface. The sound was like a muffled explosion. Kushal sighed with satisfaction as Slenderman's entire head was encompassed in a yellow and green cloud. Angel yelled from above. "Geez, Kushal. I can smell that one from here."

Hillary covered her nose with her hair and held it. "So gross. Good one, Kushal. Grab the ring."

Kushal pushed Slenderman over. The demon's blank face was olive green. Kushal tore the Talisman Ring off the chain.

"Toss it to me," Angel said as he hovered inches above Kushal. Kushal threw it to Angel who grabbed it and flew back into the woods.

"Come on, Hill. We gotta get out of here. I don't know if my gas is deadly or if Slenderman is just unconscious and will wake up and come after us."

Hillary backed down the steps carefully. "Turn around, I'll lead you," Kushal said. She took his hand, and they ran down the pathway passing all the dolls.

"That was beyond terrifying," Hillary said. "I think I'll be scarred for life."

Kushal laughed. "Nah, you'll forget all about it when we get home."

"Yeah, if we get home."

"Don't think negative thoughts. Remember the fairy said Evilla feeds off them. And we got the ring."

"So," Hillary said. "Now what do we do?"

"We have to find Evilla and kill her with kindness."

Angel met them at the end of the woods. They looked out on a green meadow with mountains in the distance. "Where do we go from here?" Kushal asked.

THE NIGHTMARE GAME

Angel patted Kushal on the back. "By the way, great job farting Slenderman to death." Angel wiped his mouth. "I got a small meal off him, but he tasted like Brussel sprouts."

"Little green balls of death," Hillary said.

Angel nodded in agreement. "I'll never look at them the same."

Kushal had his satchel open. "When I was hunting for the burrito, I thought I saw a map in here. He pulled out a folded piece of paper. "Not GPS, but maybe I can read this."

"I hope it tells us where we can find Evilla before something else tries to kill us," Hillary said.

Kushal nodded. "You got that right.

***

Kushal spread the map out on the grass. "Here's the woods," he said. As he pointed, he touched the map with one finger. "This looks like Evilla's castle." He touched a huge structure on top of mountains pictured as pointy hills on the map. "There's a path winding through the mountains. I guess we have to follow it. Looks like there's a town between us and the mountains. The path leads through it." He folded the map and put it back into the satchel.

"Great, a town," Hillary said. "What kind of people could live in nightmare world? Goblins, demons, orcs?"

"Don't forget vampires and werewolves and serial killers," Angel said. "Personally, I'm hoping for something tasty. I'm starving."

They followed the path for a short time while Angel flew over their heads. He suddenly swooped back to them landing gracefully. "Don't freak, but the path in front of us is full of poisonous snakes."

"Snakes?" Hillary said. She turned on Kushal. "This is something you're afraid of isn't it. The snakes are your nightmare."

Kushal covered his face with his hands. "I am so sorry. I've been afraid of snakes my entire life. I was born in India, you know. Cobras, vipers, asps, every nasty snake on the planet lives in India."

"So," Hillary said. "How do we get by the snakes?"

"I think I can carry one of you at a time," Angel said. "The snakes are only covering the path for a short way. There is a stream and the snakes slither in and out of it."

Kushal shuddered. "Don't tell me anymore. I'm already shaking like a leaf." He let a huge fart. The sound a blat, the green cloud hanging around his butt. Hillary grabbed Angel as she pulled hair over her nose. "Hurry and get me out of here before Kushal's gas kills us."

Angel grabbed her under her arms and lifted off the ground. "You're light. This is easy." They flew over the creek. Hillary parted her hair and looked down at the writhing mass of angry snakes. "Snakes. Why did Kushal have to be afraid of snakes?"

"What are you afraid of?" Angel asked.

"Aside from Slenderman," Hillary said. "I'm not a fan of spiders."

"Me either, but I'm much more afraid of people. When you're crippled, and in a wheelchair, people can be very cruel."

"I'm so sorry, Angel. Doesn't your father give you some support?"

"I truly believe my father wishes I was gone forever."

"That can't be true," Hillary said. "He must love you. You're all he has left."

"I wish I could believe that. He's never affectionate. He doesn't tell me he cares." Angel carefully set Hillary down close to a large rock. "You can sit here while I get Kushal."

Angel flew back to get Kushal. The overweight boy was sitting on a log eating a donut. "Want one?" He asked Angel.

"No, and you shouldn't eat one either. As it is, I'm praying I can lift you. If I can't, you'll have to try to go around the snakes on foot and wade through the creek."

Angel grabbed Kushal by the back of his plaid jacket and took off. He made it about six feet off the ground, then dropped, and dragged Kushal along. "Can't you get me any higher? My feet are touching the ground."

"Lift them up, and no, I can't lift you any higher. You weigh a freaking ton."

"The snakes will bite me."

"Not if you get your feet off the ground."

Kushal lifted his feet straight out in front of his body. Ahead, Angel spotted the creek. He tried to rise higher but couldn't. Kushal's weight kept dragging him back toward the ground.

"The snakes are going to bite me," Kushal screamed. "Go around."

But it was too late. One of the snakes launched itself high and sank its teeth in Kushal's chunky leg. Kushal shrieked and yanked the snake off his leg. The snake had already injected its venom. When Angel dropped Kushal next to Hillary, he disappeared.

"Kushal!" Hillary stood up, parted her hair and scanned the immediate area for Kushal. "He's gone. Did he die?"

"This is like a video game world. If he only has one life, he could be dead."

THE NIGHTMARE GAME

A bolt of lightning hit a tree nearby and set it on fire. Hillary looked up. She grabbed Angel and dragged him backwards as Kushal plummeted to the ground landing inches away with a huge thud. The ground shook. Kushal groaned. "What happened?"

"You died," Angel said. "Snake bite."

"But I'm back."

"We must have more than one life," Angel said. "Somewhere on our bodies there might be a life count." The three of them began searching their bodies for some indication of the number of lives they might have.

Hillary grabbed Kushal's hand. "It's not a tattoo. It's our fingers." She held up Kushal's hand. The tip of his index finger was missing. His fingernail was now attached to his knuckle. "We have three joints on each finger. Each time we die, we lose one of the joints."

"This is disgusting!" Kushal cried as he waved his short finger around. "Please do look at this." He examined his shortened finger. "Do you think when we get home, I will get my finger back?"

"If we ever get home," Angel said. "Come on. We need to get through the village. I hope there is a tasty troll or an orc I can eat."

The village was set in a small valley. A stream ran through the middle. Cottages with thatched roofs lined the narrow roads clustered around the town center. When they reached the center, Hillary gasped.

Stocks were set in the town center. Two women and a man were in the stocks, their heads clamped by wooden bars. A sign hung from each one's neck. The writing on the signs was strange and indecipherable. Weird creatures wandered the streets which were lined with small shops and open stalls selling vegetables, cooked food items, magic potions, books, and live animals like chickens and goats.

Three large orcs with fangs, no ears, bald heads and tiny eyes headed for them. Each one carried a nail-studded club. "I see lunch," Angel said and attacked one of the orcs. It squealed and fell back as Angel dragged it to the ground with his fangs embedded in the creature's neck. The other two orcs turned and ran. Angel, blood dripping from his mouth, lifted his head and hissed.

"Angel has his meal, let's run," Hillary said.

"But there is a pie shop," Kushal said. "I do love pie."

"Kushal, do you wish to die again?"

"No, I do not."

"Then hurry. Get me out of here."

Kushal grabbed her hand and led her through the town center, past a fountain spraying blood, or at least something red, down a street lined with more cottages and out of the village.

They ran out of the village and down a narrow track that led toward the mountains. Angel soon joined them. "I could live here," he said. "That orc was delicious."

"Gross," Hillary said. "Check the map Kushal and see if we're heading in the right direction. Kushal pulled it out of the satchel, turned it this way and that and looked at Hillary with a confused expression on his face. "According to this, we're almost there. I thought the mountains were a lot farther away."

They exited a thick stand of trees and found themselves at the base of a tall mountain. At the top of the mountain Evilla's castle rose like a ghastly beacon into the gloomy sky. It was built from black rock. Three tall domed towers were surrounded by a massive wall. A gate leading through the wall was guarded by smaller towers on each side. The gate itself was made of black timbers held in place with massive golden hinges and was locked and barred.

"How do we get through that?" Kushal asked.

"The Talisman Ring," Hillary said. "Where'd you put it?"

"Me? I don't have it."

"Then where is it? We got it off Slenderman."

"I have it," Angel said. He slipped the ring and the chain it hung off from around his neck and handed it to Hillary. The ring was a thick band of black metal with a strange design stamped onto the flat top.

Hillary turned it over and over. "What is this thing on the ring? I can't make sense of it."

Kushal took it and rubbed his finger over the raised design. "I think it's a spider."

"Oh Geez," Hillary said. "You're kidding?"

"I think not." Kushal turned the ring on its side so Hillary could see it. He held it in a shaft of weak sunlight. A golden spider appeared.

"I hope this doesn't mean the castle is infested with spiders," Hillary said with a shudder. "Because if it is, I just can't go in there."

"Well," Kushal said. "If we want to go home, we will have to."

They started up the road to the castle. It was a steep climb that zigged and zagged back and forth across the side of the mountain. "Stop," Kushal gasped. "I need a few minutes to get my breath."

"I'll take a recon flight over the gate and see what we're facing while you two rest," Angel said.

He flew high over the towers, circled twice, dropped into the castle itself once, then rose out from between the towers and returned. "I have good news and bad news," he said. "Which you want first?"

"Good," Hillary and Kushal said together.

"Well, from what I can see, the castle has no guards, no people at all. I did snag a glimpse of Evilla. She sits on a throne in the middle of a large court like Jabba the Hut. It looks like the bitch be alone."

"That is good," Hillary said. "So, what's the bad news?"

Angel grabbed Hillary's head and stared into her eyes. "The place be crawling with spiders. Big, hairy, ugly spiders, small skittering spiders, mama spiders covered with baby spiders. Even I felt fear."

Hillary dropped to her knees and pulled her hair over her face. "No, no, no. I can't. I'll die. We'll all die. We'll get spider bit and die a terrible death. The spiders will wrap us up in webs and suck us dry."

Angel shot Kushal a look full of meaning. "Hillary, I think we need to know your last superpower before we go up there."

"What are you talking about?" Hillary asked in a harsh voice. "How is that going to keep us from getting eaten by spiders or our souls sucked out by Evilla?"

"We won't know until we look. Lay down. We'll be quick. Just a peek and you can pull your dress back down."

Hillary moaned. "I'm in hell." But she lay on her non face and looked down at her butt and the backs of her legs. "One giggle. One chuckle, even one rude comment and it's over."

She slowly reached behind her and pulled her dress up an inch at a time. When it reached her butt, she pulled it up only until a tiny fraction of her behind was visible. "I'll lift the cheek, you guys look, and you better be fast, and tell me."

She pulled her butt cheek up. There were two lines under it not just one. "Two more powers," Angel said. "You can sing happy songs and you're immune to all kinds of venom. That's it."

Hillary yanked her dress down and got onto her knees. "That means spiders, too, right?"

Kushal nodded. "If I were to guess, I would say certainly. You should be immune to spider venom."

Hillary shuddered. "I still hate spiders. If one bites me, Imma kill it."

"Don't forget you can sing, too," Angel said. "Since neither of us can, you have to kill Evilla with happy songs."

"I don't know any happy songs."

They climbed up the steep road to Evilla's castle. It was paved with large red and black stone. As they got higher, the walls on the side of the path became taller as though the path was carved out of the mountain. The path also became narrower. It was like walking through a canyon. High above, Hillary could see a tiny spot of cloudy sky.

They reached a bridge over a rushing stream and Hillary stopped. "There's something wrong with that bridge. Look, it's fat in the middle and it looks like legs attach it to the rocks on the side of the stream."

"We have to go over it," Kushal said. "There is no other way to get to the castle."

"Couldn't you carry me?" Hillary asked Angel.

"The walls on the other side are too high and too close to the bridge. There's only a small space to pass through. I couldn't do it."

"Let us just move on and get over this thing," Kushal said.

"Sure," Hillary said. "What if it was a snake?"

"Oh, that would be an entirely different story."

He stepped onto the bridge and walked to the middle. "See, it's nothing, just a bridge. We have many at home."

Hillary walked out on the bridge and pushed Kushal. "Hurry." Then the bridge shuddered under their feet. The supports that looked like legs detached from the rocks and the bridge slowly rolled over. "No!" Hillary screamed. "It's a freaking spider."

"Black widow," Angel said as he hovered above them. "I can see the red spot on its abdomen." He swooped down and pulled Kushal off the wiggling spider to the rock ledge.

Hillary stood frozen, staring through her hair at the hideous fangs of the spider. She turned her head and saw she had three feet at least to go to get to the other side. "Help me, Angel. Pick me up."

Angel swooped low to grab her, but the spider anticipated the move, snagged Angel with her grasping arms and pulled him to her fangs. "Run," he shouted to Hillary. Hillary ran backwards to the path and grabbed a big rock. She drew a deep breath. Even though she was immune to the spider's venom, she was still terrified. They were so horrible and icky. But she had to do something to try to save Angel. He'd been grabbed while trying to save her.

She turned and backed slowly to the ledge and bashed the spider's head with her rock. It dropped Angel, but he'd already been bitten. His face swelled, and he exploded.

Hillary backed up to Kushal and grabbed his hand. "Run, get us out of here."

Kushal led her as fast as she could go up the steep slope. Since she could see behind her. She saw the spider turn and glare at them out of red eyes. The spider didn't chase them though, she turned and resumed her position as a bridge.

"If this is the only way out of here, we'll have to cross her again," Hillary said. "She's back to being a bridge."

"Where's Angel?"

The crash of lightning alerted them. They both looked up and saw Angel plummeting toward them. Instead of crashing into the path, he took off flying, circled, and landed in front of them.

He held out his right hand. His index finger was missing a joint.

Hillary hugged him. She couldn't see his face; however, she felt his gratitude. "Thanks," she said. "You gave up one of your lives trying to save me."

He patted her back. "Let's go kill this Evilla chick and get the frick out of here."

***

They quickly climbed to the massive gate. It stood twenty-feet high, towering over their heads, made of ebony wood with gold strapping and a thick bar across it. In the center was a lock, also gold, with a spot in the middle for the key. Angel took the ring in his hand. "This is it. I don't know what's on the other side. I never saw any people, just Evilla sitting on her throne."

Hillary waved her hand. "Oh, just open it. If we die, you guys have two lives left . . . I think, and I have three."

Angel fit the spider on the ring into the lock and turned it. A loud click scared Hillary. "Well, if there's anyone on the other side, they now know we're here."

Hordes of spiders appeared on top of the walls. Big hairy ones, little ones, black widows, funnel spiders, and tarantulas sat waiting for them to enter. Kushal backed away. "I know they're not snakes, but spiders are not a good thing either. All venomous creatures should be banned."

"When I open this door, they're going to swarm us," Angel said.

"Kushal, maybe your farts will help," Hillary said. "Turn around and when Angel opens the door let one rip."

Kushal closed his eyes. Hillary clearly heard his stomach burble. "Fear seems to generate the gas," he said. "And I am surely terrified right now."

"Ready?" Angel asked.

"Not really," Hillary said. "But open the damn gate anyway."

Angel pushed the heavy gate open a few inches and peered inside. "They seem to be waiting for us to step into the castle."

THE NIGHTMARE GAME

Hillary edged Angel to one side and pushed Kushal forward. "Turn around and blast them."

Kushal inched his large butt through the opening. The spiders moved toward him. Little ones crawled up his legs. Big ones landed on his back. Kushal screamed and cut the biggest fart Hillary had ever heard. It sounded like a bomb had gone off. Green and orange gas blew into the courtyard of the castle. Hillary moved Kushal further inside and stared. Spiders were everywhere and all of them were dead. The ones still alive had backed against the castle walls.

"Walk backwards," Angel said to Kushal. "When you get inside the castle, rip off another one."

Hillary grabbed Kushal's satchel and found another burrito. "Here. Eat this. You need fart fuel."

Once inside the castle itself, a path of golden tiles led up a circular staircase. "She's up there," Angel said. "The throne room is in a room at the top of those stairs."

Kushal cut another massive blast of flatulence and Angel whispered to Hillary. "Maybe you should start singing now. You go ahead of us since you're immune to the spider venom and start singing. It's what kills Evilla and it's your superpower. Kushal has done his part. Now it's your turn."

"Maybe I'm immune," Hillary sobbed. "But I still hate spiders. Look at them. Creepy, gross, eight-legged, nightmares. I'll be dreaming of this for the rest of my life."

"If we get out of here," Angel said. "And unless, you start singing, that might never happen."

A sudden breeze lifted Hillary's hair off her eyes. "I don't think we're alone," she said.

Angel rose off the floor of the castle. "Souls be here, Hillary. All the souls Evilla done sucked out of the bodies of children prolly caught in the game like us."

Ghostly apparitions swooped around them, through them, grabbing with insubstantial fingers for their bodies and hair. Hillary, Kushal. And Angel spun in circles batting at them. "What can we do?" Kushal cried.

"Nothing," Angel said. "They can't hurt us. I think they just trying to warn us. This be what Evilla do. She sucks out your soul. Start singing, Hillary, dammit. Start right now."

"Wha, what will I sing?"

"Try *You are my Sunshine*. That be a happy song. Then do *Don't worry be Happy*, and *Somewhere Over the Rainbow*. Do it."

"I really can't sing," Hillary said.

"Yes, you can. It's on your damn backside. Sing!"

THE NIGHTMARE GAME

Hillary found she knew all the words of *Don't Worry be Happy.* She sang and the ghosts swirled around them leading them up the stairs toward Evilla's throne room. Halfway up the stairs a girl appeared. She was beautiful, tall, dark hair flowing down her back.

"Who is that?" Kushal asked Hillary.

Hillary shrugged. "Don't know." She launched into *You are My Sunshine* stunned she could sing. Wouldn't it be wonderful if she kept this gift when she returned home?

Angel flew up to the girl, who lifted high with him. They hissed at each other baring fangs. "Vampire," Kushal said. "She is a vampire like Angel."

Angel and the girl circled each other. The girl wore black leather leggings, boots, and a silky black shirt. "Who are you?" Angel asked.

"I am Liliha, Evilla's daughter."

"But you're a vampire like me."

"A vampire came here to kill my mother. He found me first and turned me."

"What happened to him?"

Liliha's striking blue eyes filled with tears. "Evilla killed him."

"Just like a black widow spider," Hillary said.

Angel took Liliha's hand. "That sucks. My mother is dead. My father might be alive but he don't care about me."

"Geez," Kushal said. "Would you two please stop. We must continue up these endless stairs for which I am not physically suited and kill Evilla."

Hillary had reached the top. The staircase opened to a large room with a glass dome over it. Clouds scudded across the sky visible through the glass. Blasts of rain hit the glass creating a staccato of sound. Hillary had to expand her chest and project to make her voice heard over the rain. She sang *Somewhere Over the Rainbow* followed by *Hooked on a Feeling*. Evilla squirmed on her throne and covered her ears.

"Stop! Cease that caterwauling noise." She opened her mouth wider and wider until it was a monstrous black hole. Hillary felt the suction. Kushal began moving toward Evilla's open mouth. Hillary grabbed him and sang *Happy,* followed by The Beachboys *Good Vibrations.*

Evilla screamed again and sucked harder. Hillary had to hang onto Kushal and weigh him down. Above her Liliha held onto Angel to keep him from being sucked into Evilla's wide open mouth.

"Keep singing," Liliha yelled. Sing *YMCA* by The Village People. She hates that one the most. Then sing *I Get Around* Beach Boys."

Hillary sang louder and the suction from Evilla's open mouth lessened. She was hugely obese like a Jabba the Hut Cruella DeVille. Her white face sported heavy jowls and a thick layer of makeup. As Hillary sang one song after another, the makeup began to melt. It looked as though Evilla's entire face was melting. Ghosts flew around the room. The ghosts of children circled Evilla faster and faster.

Hillary sang *YMCA* again and Kushal, Angel, and Liliha joined in. Evilla's morbidly obese body shrank. Her dress hung from her blubbery shoulders. Clumps of flesh dripped from her face and hunks of long black hair fell out. As Hillary sang, Evilla decomposed right before their eyes.

"Noooo," she cried. "Stooooop singing."

But Hillary didn't stop. The songs made her happy. The happiness inside her filled the room. Kushal felt it. "Yes, Hillary, make the happiness go everywhere. It feels very good inside of my body."

Angel swooped over Hillary's head. "You're wonderful. I feel so light and joyful." He held Liliha's hand both of them laughing as they flew up to the dome and back to Hillary.

When Evilla had melted into a puddle of black and red goo, Hillary moved closer. She toed the pile of stinking slop with one foot while she sang *Get the Party Started,* a Pink song.

Kushal tilted the throne over. There was no more Evilla. She was dead.

***

When Kushal announced Evilla was dead, Ariel appeared with a poof. She fell onto her butt eating a hot dog. "That looks delicious," Kushal said.

"You can't have any," Ariel said. "It'll give you bad gas and kill us all."

"Have we completed the task?" Hillary asked.

Ariel's black wings fluttered, and she flew over the gross heap of Evilla glop. "She looks dead to me."

"Then we get to go home?"

Ariel held out her hand and a silvery wand appeared. Angel and Liliha landed in front of her.

"If you don't mind," Angel said. "I wanna stay here with Liliha. If I return to my chair, I think it will kill me. Here be all free and shit. I can walk, run, and even fly. And I have Liliha." The two vampires embraced.

"Will that be enough?" Ariel asked. "Will you miss your friends and your father? Will a life as a blood sucker be enough for you? Because, once you decide to stay, the only way out for you is for your friends to return to the Nightmare Game and bring you home. To do that, there will be another difficult task. One so difficult, they might die. And communications between the game and the real world are hard. I would have to give you a coin. And it can only be used once."

THE NIGHTMARE GAME

Angel stared at Liliha. "Will we be happy together?"

She kissed him lightly on the lips. "As happy as Hillary's songs."

"Imma stay," Angel said.

Ariel handed him a coin. "If you wish to go home, shine the coin until it is bright and gleaming. Hillary will have the matching one and she will see it and know you want out."

Ariel tapped Kushal with her wand and he disappeared. Hillary hugged Angel and he licked her neck. "Stop that it's gross."

Ariel handed Hillary her coin. "If the coin turns to gold, it means Angel wishes to return to his real world and his wheelchair. Will you come back for him?"

Hillary sighed. "Probably. This is the scariest place imaginable. But I think I would probably come get him."

Ariel smiled. "Then go home." She tapped Hillary on the top of her head and the next thing Hillary saw was Kushal, returned to his form. She patted her face. "My face," she sobbed. "My face is back."

They stared at Angel's empty wheelchair. Sadness filled Hillary's heart. "Will we ever see him again?"

"Not if his father catches us up here."

JANET POST

They held hands and ran out of Angel's house never once looking back.

DELIVER US FROM EVIL

Elizabeth Alsobrooks

Something is wrong.

I changed. Grew weaker. I no longer know what I should have known. I tried to pinpoint when I first noticed but couldn't. Perhaps I'd been too distracted by Harut.

All I knew now, with certainty, was that I had only a fraction of the clairvoyant ability I once took for granted. The young woman I once was, was gone.

I hadn't known her for long, but in eighteen summers the girl I used to be had learned to hone her craft and become the most powerful conjurer in her coven, and beyond. How could I fail to do so when that was my mother's intention, after all.

My mother, formidable and scheming, and motivated by nothing so much as jealousy. She bedded one of the most feared warlocks ever to arrive in Salem, hoping for what she received, an offspring with even greater potential. Falling in love with my father had not been part of my mother's plan.

But plans change. Now Isabelle Young was determined to become more than just another of his playmates. She had every intention of replacing his wife, and by whatever means were necessary.

Part of that new plan included a father who doted on his only child, me, Seraphina Alise Richards. He did. He took great pride in each new achievement. He liked to laugh and assure me that I was just like him, just like my daddy. But I had begun to see a glimmer of concern, and something more, when he praised my latest accomplishments.

My father does love me, I'm sure of it. Still, I'm confused as to why he now seems to fear me. I wonder what he saw, my loving father, this wielder of magic who amassed great wealth because of his ability to see the future. He doesn't predict it. He sees it. My father is a seer, in an age when only the wisest still believed in such magic.

I am not a seer. I don't see the future. Instead, I know things. Some would call it intuition, but it is much more than that. I know with absolute certainty that something will or will not happen. When you add my ability to make things happen, or not happen, at will, what does one call that?

Some would call me a caster or witch or magic wielder, but I call myself a conjurer. I conjured much of the world in which I live. With little more than the urging of my thoughts I can conjure whatever item, being, or event I want. If I were an evil or even a greedy mortal, I would have become very dangerous to humankind.

But I am neither.

***

So why does Damion Richards fear his own daughter?

Does it have something to do with the source of his power, Emnoful, who the foolish humans call Stephen?

When my new and very deliberately pursued *girlfriend*, Seraphina, introduced her father to me he seemed nervous and overly cordial. With little more than a suggestion, Seraphina told me her father was very pleased with her new boyfriend and told her he was satisfied at last that she had met such a well-respected man.

I chuckled at the time, not because I cared what Seraphina's father thought of me, Harut Meruik, but because of how ridiculously simple it was to load enough faux identity and background information from the dark web to make people believe it.

At the time, I assumed he was glad that she wasn't toting a gigolo on her arm. No doubt even a less decerning eye than her father's could see I'm far from average by the simple fact that I don't shop. My clothes are more than couture, they are custom made, the rare kind that brings designers to me, at my convenience.

And *my* design is to make Damion Richards accept and respect me. He is a millionaire, true, but he is not a billionaire. That is, of course, his weakness, his desire to become one. My investment financier *background* was also designed to draw him to me. Only then could I get closer to Emnoful and defeat him.

Seraphina pulled the notecard from the bouquet and smiled. The first flowers Harut sent were dominated by white lilies of the valley, which represented beauty, grace and purity. Harut sent her those after their chance meeting in the bookstore and the cup of latte and chat that followed. Next came Star Gazer Lilies, for their blossoming friendship. He sent exotic chocolates and intricately embroidered handkerchiefs and even a delicate rose made entirely of crystal.

When a man who literally had billions at his disposal sent frequent but not overly extravagant gifts, there was something that Seraphina did know, he was purposeful and thoughtful in these tokens of affection, and he had chosen them himself. That realization alone made them the most perfect gifts she ever received.

After the initial kiss, for which he surprised her by first asking permission, and a few more dates, he sent a beautiful shade of purple roses, magic. The second three dozen roses were orange, desire. But these, these most recent roses were at last red, for love.

She buried her nose amidst the fragrant buds and skipped toward the stairs. Another thing she knew was that she was head over heels in love with Harut Meruik.

At three inches above six feet, Harut was tall for someone with the appearance of Asian roots, except for the startling blue of his eyes. They seemed to almost glow from within, and when she gazed into them, she sometimes felt she could deny him nothing. That thought nagged at her, but she refused to dwell on it. Anyone in love wanted to please the recipient of their affection.

His name proclaimed a middle eastern parentage he was perpetually vague about, always managing to change the subject. Although she had easily vetted him and discovered that he was a reclusive billionaire who guarded his privacy, that secretive lifestyle meant that much about him remained a mystery.

***

I'm not used to mysteries, Seraphina reflected. I am used to knowing everything. The only thing Harut hasn't told me outright that I know despite his cagey disinterest is that he holds some sort of resentment toward his father.

If only I could conjure the reason for that resentment, I am sure it would help explain the mysteries Harut keeps hidden from me. Somehow Harut, whether consciously or unconsciously, can shield things from my knowing. Perhaps this unique ability is what I find most attractive.

Just then, as if sensing my attention, he emerged from the water and raised his hands to slick back his hair. He strode gracefully up the pool steps, looking every bit as alluring as an Armani commercial. Every female poolside had the same impression.

Apparently.

Just as he turned toward me, his smile gleaming bright from his tanned face, a young twenty something female sporting a bobbed jet-black hairdo and little else, blocked his path.

She didn't notice the sardonic lift of his eyebrows or the now fake sincerity of his smile, supported more by the clenching of his firm jaw than his recognition of her presence. But when she reached out to run her hand down all the hard eight pack muscles to slide toward the enticing skin above his low-slung boxer trunks, I held my breath in anticipation of his reaction.

DELIVER US FROM EVIL

He snatched her hand away and bent down to look her in the eyes. I didn't hear what he said, but her reaction was immediate. She spun on her heels and strode away as though she expected him to pull a Glock out of his trunks and open fire.

"Something you said?" I asked sweetly, handing him a towel.

"It's just as often what I don't say," he said, and chuckled as he took the towel with a soft, "thanks."

I watched as he dried himself. Why wouldn't I? When I reached for my robe, he moved to take it and hold it up for me to slide my arms in. There was just a moment's hesitation as he helped me into it, and I felt his attention skim down my body before he covered me in the fluffy white warmth.

"Had enough swimming for one day?"

"That and I don't think the female population of Salem can take any more of your indoor sunshine," I said, grinning up at him.

"If you're up for it, after we shower and get changed, I made us an appointment for a couple's massage and lunch on the terrace at my other hotel."

I couldn't resist laughing. "You are the only man I know who would book a room here to sleep over if you don't feel like the twenty-five-minute drive back to Boston, and to use the indoor pool. The better choice in my opinion would always be the Encore Boston Harbor because it's a five-star hotel complete with a casino and everything else that entails."

"Oh, I don't know, the Salem hotel has good scenery," he said, glancing down at my now covered body. "How else was I going to get you into a bikini without sounding like a perv?" He pulled me close and pressed a kiss to my forehead, before guiding me toward the door that led to the elevators.

It didn't slip my attention that this was the first time he'd invited me to his hotel in Boston, though we had pretty much used up all the casual dating venues Salem had to offer, unless one wanted to attend a séance or visit a graveyard after dark. Aside from meeting in the Wicked Good Books store, we hadn't ventured into the ghostly side of Salem. The magical side, however, Harut loved to talk about. It was this sort of subject he'd been seeking when our hands both reached for the same book on the history of Salem. That was in early spring, and it was now late fall.

***

Harut pretended not to see the small yawn Seraphina hid behind her hand. The spa treatments left them both feeling relaxed and comfortable. He smiled and signaled the waiter to refill her wine glass.

"Oh, no, I shouldn't. It's barely three in the afternoon."

"Fortunately, you've nowhere to be and if you're willing you can continue to allow me the pleasure of your company." He reached to place his hand over hers and said softly, "I've an entire suite upstairs. If you feel tired, there are several bedrooms from which you can choose to take a nap."

He watched for and then saw a certain look in her eye. She was beginning to wonder why he hadn't taken their relationship to the next level. He wondered too. What prevented him from sweeping her off her feet and carrying her to his bed? He hadn't been with many women, true, but it wasn't because he didn't enjoy feminine company. It's that they too often and too soon became possessive and expected more from him than he was willing to give. He was emotionally unavailable, especially with Seraphina. She was a means to an end.

She covered his hand with her free one and leaned closer to say softly, "I would love to see your suite."

Within moments they were headed up in the elevator, his arm wrapped casually around her waist. She leaned into him, her complete trust in him, her love for him, enveloping them both. But while it should have made him feel happy, perhaps even relieved or triumphant, it rubbed against his suppressed conscience until he felt raw with guilt.

***

The suite was on the top floor and very large, with more than one sitting room. We passed a hallway where I glimpsed another, smaller one. This was the main salon, its expansive windows looking out over the harbor and the ocean beyond.

"Would you care for something to drink?" Harut asked.

"Water, I think."

"Still or sparkling?"

"Still," I said, wondering why I felt nervous. I wasn't thirsty, I wanted to stall the very thing I looked forward to, being intimate with Harut.

He turned to a small bar and twisted a cap before filling a glass. It gave me a chance to take him in. I had tried before, but his essence, the way in which I somehow came to know a person's motives, intents and actions before they revealed themselves had never been available from Harut.

Until now.

DELIVER US FROM EVIL

Despite the size of the room, he filled it. His presence, no, more his essence, his very being, dominated the space. I took a deep breath, and dove deeper. My eyelids slid shut. He glowed as if from within. I opened my eyes as he turned toward me. It wasn't something I could literally see; it was more something I saw with my inner eye. It was a knowing unlike anything I ever experienced.

Without thinking, I said, "what are you?"

It vanished. Or, rather, the glow became emotion, warm, loving, reassuring. And oh, so inviting. It drew me toward him. I took the glass and set it on an end table and melted into his ready arms.

He didn't answer my question and I forgot I asked it when he instead bent down and captured my lips. And once I was able to think clearly again, I was being lifted and carried across the room into yet another hallway.

I had a moment to register a room with high ornate ceilings and dim lighting and shades of blue and gilded gold before Harut lowered me to the bed. He never lost eye contact as he said, "would you like me to stay?"

I nodded.

"You know what I'm asking?"

"Yes," I said, and reached out to touch his arm.

He moved away and pulled off my sandals, dropping them to the floor. His own shoes were soon heel-toed off and he began to unfasten his Patek Philippe, his lips parting with a soft intake of breath as I reached to unbutton my sundress.

I was wearing too many clothes. He was wearing too many clothes. He tossed his watch onto the nightstand and soon I was wearing Harut Meruik. He lifted a long limb to straddle me and held his weight off me with his forearms as he plundered my mouth with first his lips and then his tongue, probing, entwined with mine. He rose enough to give himself access to my dress buttons, following the course of his hand with his lips.

I began tugging at his shirt, impatient to see and feel his naked flesh. He sensed my urgency and knelt, pulling it over his head and tossing it to the floor. I was young but not a virgin for several years, not since I wrongly thought I'd fallen in love with the first boy who told me that he loved me. I soon realized the lie, knew it to be a wish rather than a fact, and soon that chapter of my life ended. I thought nothing more about it than that it had prepared me for moments like this.

I thought wrong. Until now I had only known one boy. Harut was all man, a gentle but aggressive male who had me naked, aroused and breathless within moments. And I loved every one of those moments.

***

I put down my phone. "My father invited us to a party tomorrow night," I said, picking up my fork and spearing a sausage link. "I know it's short notice and you have more business to conduct, so if you can't make it, I totally understand."

He kept chewing as he cast a sidelong look at me. Then he washed the bite of omelet down with milk and said, "A party? You mean with strange men and booze and one gorgeous and sexy you? I wouldn't dream of missing it." He reached out to smooth a long golden strand out of my face, the gesture simple but intimate.

I returned his smile, wondering why Stephen insisted my father invite him. How did Stephen even know about him? Did he want Harut to invest in his newest scheme? I wouldn't let Stephen or even my father try to use my relationship with Harut for financial gain. Stephen tried to pry information out of me the last time I saw him at father's. I knew nothing about Harut's conglomerate, and I wasn't going to get involved, no matter how much they tried to persuade me. But whether I liked it or not, the more questions they asked, the more I found myself wondering.

"You know, my father asked me the other day why you've never attended anything but evening activities with us. When I stopped to think about it, because it seemed so strange, I realized he was right. But then I know you have business you attend to even on the weekends, and you do things with me in the daytime. I wonder why he found it odd?"

"Are you asking me why your father is odd?"

"Very funny. There's no way we're going to waste our time with that endless topic." I'm being foolish, letting my father and his financial advisor fill my head with nonsense. If only I was able to get a better read on Harut. No, how could I doubt him after the night we shared? If I hadn't already been in love with him . . . he ruined me for all other men. I don't have to be well experienced to realize he knew his way around a woman's body, at least he left no curve unexplored on mine. At the very least, I now know the difference between a boy and a man.

I couldn't wait to explore more of his body. Now would be good.

Emnoful no doubt sensed my presence in her father's home, though I blocked him from knowing my identity or whereabouts. It must be driving him crazy, which suits me fine.

DELIVER US FROM EVIL

I can tell she is trying to figure out what is wrong. She suspects something isn't right but isn't able to put her finger on it. I have no intention of letting her know any more than she must. Certainly not that I know Emnoful, who they know as Stephen, or what he really is, and that I have known him, or of him, for thousands of years.

Not yet anyway.

***

Emnoful stood in his unlit study looking out over the water. He didn't need light to see. Darkness was his true home, the shadows his allies. He lifted his hand and a cup of Turkish coffee appeared in it. Taking a swallow, he lowered his hand and released the handle. It floated where he left it.

His life had been so much easier in the old world, in ancient times. Dozens, even hundreds of mortals could go missing before anyone noticed. They were little more than cattle, back when his kind ruled the world.

"We will again," he pledged.

A knock sounded. He willed the door to open, and said curtly, "Enter."

"You sent for me, My Lord?"

"She's back."

"She?"

"That bastard thinks he can fool me. Well, I might not be able to find him, but he can't disguise his presence. Not since she returned. Of course, he would find her, seek her out. Such a fool." He laughed, but there was no humor in it. "He doesn't even recognize her. But I did. I saw her photograph in Genii, that foolish rag the magic users read. She stood next to her father, and even though she was not facing the camera I would have recognized her anywhere. I meant to seek her out a little later. It's not like I didn't know where she was, after all. It didn't move my timeline up by much though. No matter what, he will do anything to keep her safe. Even now. She's the perfect bait."

"He?"

"Pay attention, fool! Harut! I may not be able to kill him, but there are worse things than dying. Come closer. I have an errand for you."

***

Disgusted with simpering women, I extricated myself from yet another annoyance, and headed toward the entrance doorway, where I knew Masao waited.

Finding him in the foyer, I said, "Something feels off. She's forty minutes late and not answering her cell. Check to see if Seraphina is still at home getting ready."

"Right away. I'll send someone."

I nodded and the well-dressed slender Asian who acted as my assistant, and driver, stepped out the front entrance to make a call.

"Oh dear, our princess hasn't arrived yet, I see," Damion said from behind me.

I turned to my host with my best social smile in place. "I should have picked her up, but she insisted on meeting me here. No matter. The wait is aways worthwhile."

"Indeed. Thanks for coming on such short notice. Seraphina's friends, and mine, have heard so much about you, I felt it was time to satisfy their curiosity."

"Of course," I said, seeing his lie for what it was.

"Ah, here at last," Damion said, reaching his hands out to capture those of a platinum bombshell bearing down on us, who if her gorgeous figure and symmetrical features were any indication, had to be Seraphina's mother. He looked past her and asked, "Isn't Seraphina with you?"

"What? She's not here?" The woman looked around the crowded room. "She left before I did. She should be here by now."

"Perhaps there was car trouble. I'll just go check," I said before bolting from the room and out the front door.

Seeing Masao on his phone, near the valet, I rushed forward. "Anything?"

"She took a cab but wasn't headed this way. She was headed toward Boston. That's all we have so far. We're pulling all the surveillance footage."

"In the meantime, let's get to Boston! There's no way she would head off to Boston after inviting me here. I knew there was a problem. I felt it. I should have intervened sooner."

***

"That's not your I'm happy to see you look, Seraphina," Emnoful taunted.

"Stephen, where's Harut? What are you doing here?"

"I assume he's at your father's party about now."

"What are you talking about? I got a message saying he'd been in an accident and was being treated by a doctor who was a friend of his. I'm supposed to be meeting him here."

"You will. He will be along soon. I am here waiting to see him too. Let's have a cup of coffee while we wait." He waved his hand toward a low table next to a sofa. Two cups of coffee with a sugar bowl and creamer awaited them."

"I don't want any damn coffee, Stephen." She pulled her phone out of her purse and pressed. A moment later she made a sigh of frustration. "Why isn't this ringing?" She looked down at it and said, "How is there no signal here? We're in Boston, not the middle of nowhere."

"I know, frustrating, isn't it? Please, have a seat," Stephen said, indicating the sofa, while he sat in an adjacent chair.

"No, I'm leaving. I'm going to my father's and find out what's going on with Harut."

Stephen chuckled. "Okay, I guess we do this the hard way," he said. He snapped his fingers and Seraphina dropped to the floor, unconscious.

***

"You've made another bad choice, Emnoful."

"At least I'm capable of making a choice, Harut. Oh, wait, you have made a choice, and it's not bad, really. I mean if you like that sort of creature. She looked very lovely tonight, her hair piled on top of her head with just a few golden curls brushing against her shoulders. And those emeralds really set off the color of her eyes."

"How would you like to spend the next few thousand years on the bottom of the ocean?" Harut asked, smiling.

"You keep this up and you're going to fall from grace again, daddy's boy."

Harut took a step forward.

"Ah, watch it. You wouldn't want Layla to come to any harm, would you? I mean, not again."

"What are you—"

"It only just dawned on you who she is. Yes, it's her. I recognized her immediately. You knew it too, if you admit it to yourself."

"What I did or didn't know is of no concern of yours. Where is she, Emnoful?"

"Closer than you might think. Ah, the wards we had to put up to keep you from knowing."

"Don't harm her," I ordered, my voice thick with rage and concern even to my own hearing. "It's me you want."

"That's not entirely true." Emnoful took a swallow of his coffee. He set it down and said, "The fact that I recognized her, I mean they could be twins, Harut, is only part of the reason I came here. You and I both know I want her power. You kept her from me before, but not this time. This time she belongs to me."

"You think you could live a thousand years without further sustenance, with the power of her essence. But you are very mistaken, Sparky. You would never live long enough to enjoy it."

Emnoful spang to his feet. "Careful, bat boy. I got you here to negotiate, but if you're going to be insulting you know who's going to suffer for it."

***

I awoke and stared at the ceiling, wondering where I was. I wrinkled my nose against an unpleasant, pungent smell. It smelled like rotten eggs. Sulfur? I felt queasy. My head throbbed. I blinked and then remembered. Stephen. I sat up and pressed a hand to my forehead. It didn't ease the pounding.

I swung my feet off the bed, frowned when I saw the spent syringe on the nightstand, and stood. The room faded out, and I pressed my hand against the mattress to steady myself. Back in focus, the door came into view. I rushed to push down on the lever, only to find it locked. It occurred to me as I raised my hand to pound on the oak panel that it wasn't a good idea to let Stephen or whoever else might be on the other side of the door know that I was awake.

Instead, I turned to scan the room for another way out. The window! Sprinting across the room, I pushed back the drapes and looked out. I was on the third or fourth floor. But there was a ledge and somewhere nearby there had to be a fire escape.

The window opened without sound or difficulty. After ducking my head out and seeing no visible fire ladders in either direction, it was a little trickier to quiet my panic and step onto the ledge. It was wider than my foot by about three inches. Doable, I told myself, cursing aloud that my magic wouldn't work for some reason.

The building was sided with brick, so I was able to dig my fingertips into the grout lines as I edged along. I headed left, which let my dominant hand hold onto the windowsill firmly while I began my perilous journey.

"Bless the darkness," I said softly. It was too dark to see the sidewalk below me from this height. Even so, I refused to look down as I focused on finding a fingerhold and then inching along a few inches until I had to stop and regroup, starting the process again. It took what seemed like hours, though I knew it was only minutes, for me to reach another window. It was dark inside, so I cautiously tried to push it up without losing my balance. Locked. Dammit.

Another eternity and I realized I had reached a corner. I edged my toe around the ledge, thankful to discover the ledge continued. Easing around the corner, I glanced down. It was much darker below. It must be an alley. Perhaps there would be a fire escape. My heart beat faster in anticipation.

Just ahead I saw another window, but this one had lights shining from within. I slid my left foot along the ledge until it rested against the bottom of the windowsill, then pulled my right foot close enough to allow me to lean over and peer inside. There were sheers that obscured the room's interior, but I could make out two men. Their voices rose, in the heat of an argument.

I leaned in to listen and heard Stephen's voice. Fear made me pull back. The question of whether he was still outside the room he'd locked me in was answered. What I wanted to know now was why. What probable reason could my father's financial advisor have to kidnap his daughter? The criminal behavior that resulted in this act of desperation must be bad, but what? Had he embezzled money from my father? It seemed unlikely since my father claimed he'd made a killing with Stephen's help. But perhaps Stephen helped my father so he could then help himself. Or what if my father saw something Stephen didn't want him to. The only silent witness was a dead one. But that would mean he intended to kill me, too.

Just then I heard Harut's voice. "If you dare to touch so much as a hair on her head, Emnoful!"

Who was Emnoful? Was he talking to Stephen or was someone else in the room? Had Stephen lied to us about his identity? And if so, why did Harut know who he really was? Wait, Harut never met Stephen. So, once he did, once he came here looking for me, did he recognize him as someone else, someone he had known in the past?

I must know. Leaning sideways, I pressed my face as close to the window as I could while still clutching the windowsill and keeping my balance. Just then a flash of lightning illuminated the sky, and the crack of thunder made me clutch at the windowsill to keep from falling. Rain. That's all I needed. I had to get to safety.

A glance inside as I began to move further down the ledge made me cry out in surprise. One of the men reached a hand toward the window. Even through the blurring of the sheers, I saw his form burst into flame. Then, fire, blue and white from the intensity of the heat shot toward me. Displaced air shattered the glass in front of me and I nearly vomited at the stench of sulfur before the explosion propelled me backward. Then I saw a flash of something else, golden and blinding, and I lost my bearings. My hands were torn away from the window frame, and I screamed.

DELIVER US FROM EVIL

I fell toward my death with increased velocity. Unable to even turn my head, I closed my eyes and waited for the coming impact.

But then familiar arms, strong and comforting, wrapped around me. One arm tucked under the back of my knees while the other supported my back. Somehow Harut broke my descent. Instead of downward, we rose upward, at an even more terrifying speed.

From somewhere below, I heard Stephen scream, "This isn't over, Harut!"

I managed to pry my eyes open against the wind velocity, enough to focus on Harut, head turned skyward.

How? I wondered.

Even as I saw the how, I couldn't believe it.

Harut carried me in his arms and flew, with wings so beautiful and magical I could barely breathe. He radiated light until he glowed as if he himself were a power source of unimaginable supremacy.

He glanced down at me then, his cerulean eyes filled with concern and still as bright and full of promise as a spring morning. Leaning down, he pressed a kiss to my forehead. I tried to smile but couldn't keep my mouth from gapping in awe.

My eyelids slid shut again, and I sighed. I relaxed against him. Safe. Protected. Cherished.

Something bad had happened, but I couldn't quite remember exactly what.

We began to descend. I couldn't tell where we might be. He didn't set me down but carried me into some sort of warehouse.

Where was I again? How did I get here?

It wasn't until Harut ran up a flight of stairs that I realized it was a hanger, and we had just boarded a private jet.

"Wh-what? Where are we going?"

"Portugal. I need to draw Em--Stephen back to Europe and away from your family."

"Stephen? That's right. He kidnapped me. You saved me, didn't you?"

"I will always save you, Seraphina."

"Do you think he'll hurt my mother or father?"

"No, it's us he wants, so he'll follow us, but it's going to take him a while to find us and by then I'll be ready for him. You need to get some sleep. There's a bedroom at the back. Come on. I'll hold you until you fall asleep and when you wake up, I'll have more information for you. Deal?"

"Do I have any choice?"

"No."

I shrugged. The effects of whatever Stephen did to knock me out, the anxiety of thinking I was about to be killed, and everything in between . . . what exactly happened in between? Why couldn't I remember? I must still be in shock. This was probably some post trauma effect. Whatever happened, it left me exhausted. Feeling safe in Harut's arms sounded like all I could manage for now. I followed him to the back of the plane.

***

"He boarded her father's plane. Their flight plan gives the destination as Cairo."

"Good. He thinks I have taken her to home base. It will take him a while to figure out we're not in Egypt. He doesn't know about my connections in Portugal."

"He can't have ever been to Madeira, My Liege."

"Once again, please stop using titles and honorifics. There is no hierarchy here."

"Little need, when there are none who outrank you."

"Nearly all outrank me now, Masao. What was it that King David said? How the mighty have fallen. We are fallen, Masao. All that is left for us is atonement. In the end, all will outrank us."

"We can't know that. And what about Emnoful and his kind? Do you think they will be forgiven?"

"Who can tell? They serve the purpose they were given."

"As do we."

"I have never considered it that way. Let's hope you're right." I glanced toward the back. "She'll awaken soon."

Masao looked past me. "You have only two choices. You tell her the truth. All of it. Or you keep her sleeping while you carry her in."

I sighed and brushed my hair from my face. "It's not inevitable that she must know."

"She didn't know before, and knowing might have saved her life."

"Had I known the magic I taught her would attract his attention, I could have protected her."

"At least the child was saved," Masao said.

"Are you certain there was a child? We searched everywhere but found no trace."

"Her family protected it well. They hid him even from you."

"I never believed. I couldn't live with the thought of him. No, that's not quite true. I lie to myself when I say so. Until I saw Seraphina, I didn't let myself believe." How many years had it been since I held Layla in my arms? That too was forbidden. It only added to my list of sins. Would I ever know again what it felt like to live without guilt? "We could use a host to protect her, until I deal with Emnoful once and for all. Who knows how many minions he's gathered over the millenniums, with promises to retake power. He must know there are more than enough of us to prevent that from ever happening. That, and the constant infighting between their clan and the royal family."

"My sources are saying he hopes to trigger the Apocalypse," Masao said.

"Fool that he is." I glanced out the window. It would be dawn soon. "We're landing. For now, I'll just get her to safety under the cover of darkness. Have our brethren meet us in the usual place. I'll get there as soon as I can."

"I've sent Ramiel and Sareth to meet you. It's been blessed and anointed again."

I nodded. Everyone knew what was at stake. There would be no mistakes.

***

My arm was cold, so I pulled it under the down duvet and turned onto my side. Harut put his arm around me and snugged against my back. Soon I felt toasty and turned so I could gaze up at him.

He smiled and ran a long finger along the bridge of my nose.

"Morning, love," he said softly.

"I like waking up next to you," I said, and realized I would love to do it every day for the rest of my life.

He bent down to kiss my forehead and said, "I'm afraid I will have to be leaving for a while."

"Leaving? I turned my head and then looked around the room. "What the hell?" The walls and even the ceiling was made of stone. Not masonry stone, solid rock. Was this house built into the side of a mountain? "Where are we?"

"Madeira, Portugal."

"Portugal? How long have I been out, and why don't I remember anything but being kidnapped by Stephen, rescued by you, and then boarding a plane?"

"I assume Stephen drugged, you, Seraphina. You were terrified, barely coherent, and passed out as soon as I got you onto the bed. You didn't wake up when I took you to the car and brought you here. Here is where we are because you will be safe here. Stephen couldn't get to this place even if he knew it existed. Few know it exists, and those that do work for me."

I pointed to the walls and said, "And what exactly is this place? It looks to be carved into a mountain."

"It is. It's a series of caves."

"Okay, so I don't know where Madeira is. I do know where Portugal is, but the closest I've been is Spain. How did you possibly know about caves that no one else does?"

"The knowledge was passed down through those who hid to avoid religious persecution."

"Like in ancient times?"

"Ancient is relative. Look, I really hate to rush you, but I must go deal with Stephen. There's warm clothes for you there, in that armoire. It's chilly here. This room doesn't have enough ventilation for a kerosene heater. But it never gets below 62. I'm sure you're hungry, so as soon as you're dressed, you can eat. I'll go ahead and tell the others you're awake."

Harut sat up and pulled the duvet back. I noticed for the first time that he was fully dressed, except for his shoes which he bent over to put on. I wondered if he got any sleep at all.

He stood and said, "I'll get breakfast started," before moving to pull open the door and exit, closing it behind himself.

Well, it might be a series of caves, but they have done a lot of renovation. The furniture was old but well built, and there was a plush angora rug on the floor to help ward off the chill. It was done up much the same as those old castles, with a big rug on the wall behind the bed, again, to hold back the chill.

I was wearing my chamise and underwear and what I assumed was one of Harut's shirts. It made for a nice nightshirt, but I needed to get into some warmer clothes. I looked around for my cell, and remembered Stephen took it. I also needed to borrow Harut's before he left so I could call my parents and make sure they were okay. And let them know I was okay, and that they should avoid Stephen at all costs.

I dressed quickly, glad for the fleece lined pants and hoodie, along with a long-sleeved tee. Socks and lined calf boots were also provided, and I was surprised to see some fingerless gloves in the little drawer at the bottom of the armoire, along with some clean underwear. Who bought these things? It didn't seem like a man, even one as considerate as Harut would think to do so.

My stomach rumbled and I realized I hadn't eaten since yesterday afternoon. But first I needed to find out what one used as a bathroom in this series of caves.

***

"We won't be coming back until this problem has been resolved for good, Sareth."

She nodded but looked grim.

"You have to know that's the only solution," I said, knowing I didn't need to persuade her. Perhaps I needed to assuage my ever-mounting guilt. I already broke so many of the *Thou Shall Nots.*

DELIVER US FROM EVIL

Ramiel said softly, "It's much too late coming. He has had thousands of years to change, to stop his crimes against humanity, his single-minded quest to take back what he believes is rightfully his."

"Yes, I believe Lex Luther had similar ideas," I said, trying to lighten the mood. Seraphina needed to feel calm and confident, not frightened and desperate. She had to feel content because I needed her to stay inside the caves. They were blessed, protected with runes and other more ancient safeguards put in place to prevent Emnoful and his kind from entering. One doesn't need a church to have holy ground.

We all turned as Seraphina entered the large cavern that served as the main living quarters. She looked around, getting her bearings. This room was where all meals were prepared and eaten. It was heated, with lights strategically placed to make it seem more like a sanctuary than a hideout or storage facility. I would show her the rooms of relics and forgotten books and scrolls later. The remnants of my past would keep her occupied in a modern time of cell phones, internet, television, and digital music. None of which she had here.

I spent more than enough time here to create a livable environment. Although far from lux-urious, it was cozy in an escape from reality kind of way.   There was fresh water from a nearby waterfall, a small generator, and all the privacy one could wish for because technology would never find this place, thanks to the canopy provided by eight-hundred-year-old laurel trees and its designation as a UNESCO World Heritage Site. Not even they knew about this labyrinth of tunnels and caverns because its foliage-hidden entrance was further guarded by magic older than this island.

"Something smells good," Seraphina said. She noticed Sareth piling sausage onto a platter and said, "another woman."

I rose to make the introductions. Leave it to Masao to realize she would be more comfortable with at least one other female present. She would like Sareth. Ramiel's soft-spoken charm would help keep her calm, too.

***

"He will leave the rental house soon. I sense his intent. He waits for the full night. The fact that he knows he can't hide from me hasn't changed his plans. That can only mean he has a large force that has not yet crossed over," I said, stating the obvious to myself.

Masao nodded. "They no doubt have a point of entry chosen. Do you have a sense of it yet?"

DELIVER US FROM EVIL

"He's going to meet them here, in the Laurisilva Forest, away from too much interference."

"By interference you mean digital proof of their existence before they're ready." Masao slammed his fist again the tree upon which he leaned and then jumped away as sparks flew and the shattered pulp exploded."

"Not the low profile I was hoping for, Masao."

"Sorry."

It's time, I said, but no longer out loud. *Get ready*. I communicated telepathically to the fifty or so of my present brethren, collectively numbering in the thousands, and known as the fallen, like me, who retained by acts of goodness some of our former power. These few earth-bound beings fought against evil, and rather than joining the jinn or the damned to regain some of their former glory, they fought against the ifrit of the jinn alongside me.

Masao, who now functioned as my general, reminded the other soldiers that the ifrit are from one of the highest-ranking jinn, and were once the ruling nobles, so they are both powerful and arrogant, intending to rule the earth once more. Above all, they are not predictable. So don't ever underestimate them, Masao urged, even if like Harut you are a Seraphim or still possess much of your magical powers. Remember, don't try to confront Emnoful alone. He will be looking for Harut so will come in his true form and be at his most formidable.

"I plan on finding him first," I said. Raising my head, I scented the air. Sulfur. "They've begun entering from the other plane," I warned. "Emnoful and his personal guard will be here momentarily." I lifted my arm. A sword appeared in my right hand, runes and holy words of power gleaming like molten gold down its length as the sword ignited. Unlike the jinn, the sword put off smoke.

I stilled, tense with anticipation. I felt the combat-ready state of my brethren, smelled the heightened stench of sulfur in the air, and then they were upon us. Flashing forward, I felled a lesser ifrit with a flick of my sword. The holiness with which it infused his body sent him injured and defeated back to the dimension from which he had come.

Flames erupted around me, the trees bearing the brunt of the ifrit assault.

A bolt of power-infused molten rock shot toward me. I ducked. It missed. I spun around and beheld two ifrit bearing down on me. Masao, on my right flank, battled a powerful ifrit. His sword slashed out, but the monstrous being easily bent away from the strike.

Before I could see more, I lifted my sword to bash away another attack. The sparks reflected off the charmed shield I extended to include Masao before hurtling myself three feet ahead to engage the snarling pair of ifrit now shooting laser-like streams of fire from each of their four extended hands. Their faces were hideous distortions of their natural beauty, intended to strike fear that eroded confidence in their enemies. Skin as grayish black as char but as shiny as polished obsidian contrasted with the veins of molten fire swirling just beneath the surface.

"Turn back from your fool's errand and I will spare you further agony," I offered, knowing they would refuse.

The explosions that followed shook the ground for miles. Only the spells cast earlier prevented the humans all over the island from realizing the intense war taking place.

In an instant I battled eight swords, one extending from each of their hands. I didn't fear defeat, not from these lesser creatures, but it took a toll on my energy. Theirs too, I noted. With a parry, another and a thrust, I sent the first back. The other became more desperate, and more careless. I cut off his arm. He faltered, but the appendage began to reappear, oozing molten matter. As I doubled my efforts, he began to retreat.

I pressed forward, causing him to retreat again.

But then, I felt a searing pain in my upper arm. I glanced to my left and saw that another ifrit, a more powerful one, penetrated the shield with a slow, steady thrust and had I not jerked away from the pain, would have caused more severe damage. Golden light gleamed from the cut on my arm, and then a reddish hue signaled the healing had begun.

Once again, I fought against a pair of them, but the first was near exhaustion, so I concentrated my attacks on him, while slashing defensive blows against the other. Soon I was able to dispatch the first.

A rending sound signaled the breach between dimensions, and he disappeared back into his own plane. I didn't need to watch to know it automatically sealed behind him. My wound sealed too by the time I sent the other ifrit after him.

I turned to see Masao defeat his current foe, and we ran forward together to help our brethren. At least an hour passed before only a few ifrit remained. Masao and I quickly dispatched another, together, when Ishmael approached.

"We knew you wanted to confront Emnoful yourself, but he appeared and attacked us, so we banded together and took him down. We tried to detain him, but he disappeared through a rift."

"Was he badly injured?"

Ismael nodded.

"You're sure?"

"He dripped from so many wounds he looked like an erupting volcano. He limped toward the opening before someone dove through and darted back with his body. There's no way he will live."

"Unfortunately, there are many ways he could live, but he won't heal for some time if he was as badly injured as you say," Masao said.

"Let's hope you're right," I said.

No ifrit remained. Once Emnoful departed, the few stragglers that lingered soon followed him. Exhausted as we were, before we could leave the burning forest, we had to heal and restore it. Only a few of us had the power to do so. Without discussion, we began to cast some of the most powerful spells we knew.

***

"Where am I now?" Seraphina said softly, seeing me seated beside her. She looked around and said, "In a church?"

"Holy ground. Emnoful can't come here."

"He can't come here. Is Emnoful the man I know as Stephen? I thought you said you defeated him. I assumed that meant dead."

"He is not a man, but yes, you call him Stephen. We thought he was defeated but quite obviously we were wrong."

"Not a man? He can't walk on holy ground. Do you mean he's a demon?"

"No, he's not a demon. Here, once you're fully awake I'll explain. I need to come up with a plan that includes keeping you safe. First, let's be sure you're alright. Are you injured? I shielded you as best I could, but there was so much glass coming from every direction." Without waiting for her answer, he began running his hands over her limbs, then gently grasped her chin and tilted her face first one way and then the next.

"I'm sure I have a few cuts and bruises. The windows shattered right in front of me." I grasped his hand and pulled him toward me. "Could you please just hold me a little longer? I-I'm confused and frightened. I seem always to be waking up in another place with no memory of how I might have gotten there. I awoke in a car just in time to see it practically explode, as if a bomb were thrown at it. I don't even know where we are, or how I ever got in that car!"

I shivered, suddenly cold.

DELIVER US FROM EVIL

He frowned and shrugged out of his jacket. "You're in shock. Of course, you are. Here." Harut put the coat over my shoulders, sat beside me and pulled me into his arms. "Oh, wait, just a moment. I saw a water dispenser back there. Let me get you some. You're probably dehydrated, too. I don't want you to end up in the hospital."

I had no intention of leaving his side, so I stood and followed him back down the hallway. In truth I was extremely thirsty and gratefully took the cone cup he filled from the water cooler and downed it in a few big gulps. He refilled it and led me back to the bench.

"Okay, so please tell me what's going on?"

"I'll tell you what I can, sweetheart. I'm not sure where to begin."

"How about telling me why Stephen or whoever he is can't come into a church but he's not a demon."

"He's not a demon, because there are no such things as demons."

"Hold on. I wasn't raised in a traditional church, but I'm pretty sure most religions believe in demons."

"Actually, a large portion of the earth's peoples believe in three beings created by God, but demons are not one of them."

"Wait. What? What three beings are there then?"

"There are angels, humans and jinn."

"Jinn, but no demons?"

"If he's not a demon, why can't he come into a church?"

"Well, he can, and we will actually be bringing him here, but he won't want to."

"I feel like we're playing hide and seek with the truth here, Harut. Now that I'm awake, I am beginning to remember some things, like me asking you what *you* are, and you not answering me. You want me to believe in jinn, and you want me to believe there are no such things as demons. That's a pretty big stretch."

"Many believe it. You once knew it to be true but were made to forget."

"Why? By whom? By you?"

"No, by Emnoful."

"Why?"

"Because if you regained all your memories, you would know what he did to you."

I gasped and sat back down on the bench. Harut sat down and would have drawn closer, but I held my hand out, stopping him. I studied his face, dark with shadows, except his eyes. Even in the dim lighting, his eyes shone, the blue luminescent.

"What? What did he do to me, Harut?" Please don't say he raped me. Not that. Please don't let it be that.

"He sucked your very essence from your body. Had I not arrived in time to stop him, he would have ingested all that you are, and you would no longer exist. Even your soul would have perished."

"Come on, Harut. Let's say I believe in jinn, and I probably do given my family's powerful magic abilities, but magic or no, how could he suck my soul out of my body?" I felt unsettled and fought a sudden urge to run around screaming. I had slept so much throughout this, unnatural sleep. Surely, I would wake up from this nightmare and find it was all a dream.

"It's not a dream, Seraphina."

"How did you know I was thinking that? Can you read my mind?"

"I don't usually do so, respecting your privacy, but I'm very worried about you, and your rising panic shows on your face."

He ignored my raised hands and sat closer, putting his arm around my shoulders. Despite myself, it calmed me. I felt less like screaming and more like burrowing into the warmth and comfort he offered. He pulled me into his arms and rested his cheek against the top of my head as though he too needed comfort. I was still digesting the fact that he could read my thoughts and wondered if he could read the thoughts of others as well.

"Yes."

"Dammit."

"Sorry."

"I assume your friends are out looking for Emnoful. What will they do when they find him?"

Harut sighed and ran his hand through the thick tuft that liked to drive us both to distraction. Him because it fell into his eyes and me because it looked sexy as hell doing it.

"This is going to take too long. Let me just give you back what was taken." With that, he placed a hand on either side of my head and my eyelids felt like lead. I closed them, and a sudden rush of images, of moments I knew belonged to me, flashed in rapid succession through my mind. The more images I saw, the more emotional I felt. Joy, sadness, anger, despair, I experienced them all.

When they stopped, I realized Harut hadn't given me new memories, he somehow released memories that were there all along, but had been suppressed like those of an extreme trauma victim. I realized, too, that I *had* been the victim of extreme trauma, because of Emnoful, who would never again be Stephen to me.

Harut reached for a box of tissue on a nearby table, and I took one to stem the tears pouring down my face. I blew my nose and pulled myself together enough to say, "how long ago was that, were we? How is it possible that I'm here with you now, when Emnoful killed me then?"

"The when doesn't matter, though it was thousands of years ago. The how is more important. Emnoful is a soul eater. I taught you magic not because I was tasked to bring it to mankind, but because you already had the power inside you. The magic within you was strong, even then. Now, because Emnoful has been feeding power to both you and your father, it is even stronger. He wanted your power to grow because he wants it back. He wants what he could not get before."

Harut jumped to his feet. "They're here. Stay, where you'll be safe," he commanded before he moved, so quickly he literally disappeared.

I ran in the direction he took and when I came to a door, I opened it. Then closed it. A janitor's closet. The next door I opened revealed light so bright I squinted my eyes and closed the door partway until I was able to acclimate to the vision of a half-dozen angels forcing a screeching Emnoful onto the altar. I knew them to be angels, because no human could hold him, and their clothes were tattered from his claws, wounds exposed when slashes of light appeared through their skin, first golden, and then red as it healed, and the wounds stopped bleeding light. Angels, made of light, humans from clay, and jinn from smokeless fire. I remembered it all. Hell didn't host demons, it hosted damned angels who turned against their Maker, refusing to honor humans.

The screams grew so deafening, I wedged my foot in the door so I could jam my hands over my ears. No matter what, I was going to watch this vile creature's demise just as he once watched mine. A burning rage against what he had done to me, to us, Harut and I, still lingered with those long-ago memories.

Harut appeared, a large holy water stoup in his hands. Emnoful turned his head and shrieked, "Do you dare, you bastard son, fallen from your Father's grace? They will come for you, my entire clan. And for her! he added, looking over to glare at me." With a mighty effort he tore his arm from an angel's grasp and sent a bolt of fire toward me.

I ducked out of the doorway. Once the wood stopped splintering and began to burn in earnest, I hurried into the sanctuary and stooped behind a pew, determined to see his demise.

The angel recaptured Emnoful's arm, his battle evident in the slashes of light pouring from his face. Harut immediately dumped the font onto the monster's face, and then slowly poured it down the length of his body. The screaming stopped mid-screech and the silence that followed felt thick with tension. First the grayish flesh withered and began to crumble away. The fire sizzled and steamed, and dissolved. The stench was overwhelming. I wondered how the angels could stand to be so close. Finally, what was left of Emnoful, ashes and soot, suddenly vanished.

I rose from my crouched position and plopped onto the pew behind me, emotionally exhausted but immensely relieved. The angels genuflected, heads bowed, and prayed. Harut once told me he wasn't sure his Lord still heard their prayers, but though they had fallen from grace, they still loved Him and were devoted to carrying out His good will toward men.

Tears flowed from my eyes, but through them I watched with awe and crossed myself before I too lowered my head. I still felt guilty over being the cause of Harut's fall from grace. Not personally, but theoretically. I once again was able to remember what Harut told me, thousands of years ago. When warfare broke out in heaven, and a third of the angels joined with Satan, they were defeated and damned to hell. Only a few thousand refused to fight against either God or their beloved brethren and instead chose to protect humankind, fearing that such a war might result in their annihilation. They were those angels who had lived among mankind. Since they did not take a side, however, they had fallen from their Lord's grace. The shame weighed heavily upon those who still tried to do good and fight against evil.

I looked up when I felt Harut sit beside me.

"It is finally done," he said simply.

"He still hears your prayers, you know."

"Perhaps. But I can never be forgiven for something I can't bring myself to repent."

"What's that?"

"You." He bent down and pressed a warm kiss upon my lips. It was filled with love so tender and pure I couldn't fathom how it could possibly be sinful.

He pulled away and said, "Emnoful bragged to Ismael about how you came to return. He kept, all this time, that little grain of your soul that makes you different from all other humans, the spark of life given to each human upon conception. He placed it into your mother's womb. He seemed to think it was quite clever. That, and the name he put into your mother's head, to taunt me."

I shivered and drew in a deep breath, feeling a chill run up my spine.

"Have no fear of it. Every spark of life is created by none other than the Creator. No other being has such power."

"Still, to think that monster had my very soul in his possession. It makes me feel unclean."

"No, love, your soul is beautiful. Your good-ness is what first drew me to you. I feel so blessed to have you with me again. Let's forget about Emnoful and enjoy every moment we've been given."

I smiled then, happier than I ever remembered being, then or now. "Let's go home," I said.

"Wherever you are will always be home to me."

We exited the church to see a bright sunrise before us. Daybreak.

I glanced down and saw Masao sitting in the driver's seat behind the Spirit of Ecstasy, gleaming against the sleek black of the vehicle. I smiled. Harut took my hand as we ran toward him down the steps. Our new life had just begun.

Neither of us noticed the monk who passed us as he hurried up the church steps. We were in the car before he dashed down the hallway. He stooped to retrieve a paper cone cup from the wastebasket beside the bench. He grimaced as steam began to rise from his grayish flesh. Cursing, he slipped the cup into a plastic baggie and shoved it into the folds of his stolen cowl before running into the sanctuary. He dove into a waiting portal. It closed behind him. The smell of sulfur took a while longer to disappear.

ABOUT THE AUTHORS

Elizabeth Alsobrooks

Elizabeth loves New Orleans! Above she visits the tomb of the Voodoo Queen. She currently lives at the foot of the beautiful Santa Catalina Mountain Range in AZ. These days, she divides her writing time between urban fantasy, horror, and nonfiction. Work on her Illuminati series continues, but she loves throwing out horror shorts on occasion. She grew up with a love for Dante, Shakespeare, Chaucer, Poe, Hardy, Dickens, the Bronte sisters, Koontz, World Mythology, and she has even read the first novel ever written (The Tale of Genji, all 1200 plus pages), so her taste is as eclectic as her range. Find out more about her at:

www.elizabethalsobrooks.com

Shawn D. Brink

Shawn Brink (writing under Shawn D. Brink and Shawn David Brink) resides in Eastern Nebraska, U.S.A., and is represented by Liverman Literary Agency. He's building a following with a growing list of novels (mainly speculative fiction), as well as shorter works published in various publications and anthologies. Check out his website to learn more:

https://shawnbrinkauthor.wordpress.com/

Janet Post

Janet is a self-proclaimed military brat from Hawaii. She worked as a reporter for years before retiring to write books in FL. Horses and dogs are her passion along with writing adventure for young adults.

Francesca Quarto

Francesca is part of a large Italian family where she discovered early on that a love of reading was as much a part of her DNA as her mother's skill at baking.

Francesca has worked in local television, a small city zoo, founded a non-profit tutoring agency for an inner-city neighborhood which eventually served local school districts, worked for an International Evangelical Television and Radio Station and for a non-profit organization serving challenged adults. She resides in a small town outside of Indianapolis, Indiana with her husband Patrick. She still has a great love of the written word and while she enjoys her E-Reader immensely, she still treasures the excitement of turning the next page.

Darren Simon

Darren Simon has been a writer for much of his life. His career has included working as a journalist in Los Angeles, Israel and Southern California along the Mexican and Arizona borders. He presently works in government affairs on California water issues, teaches college English for the California Community College system, and does free-lance writing for regional magazines. His work as an author focuses on middle grade and young adult readers to inspire them to read the way he was inspired, first by comic books and then the science fiction and fantasy novels that were so important to his youth. He resides in California's Desert Southwest with his wife and sons.

Visit his website
at:www.darren.simon.com

Rob Tucker

Author and retired business and management consultant in a wide range of industries throughout the country, Rob resides with his wife in Southern California. He is a graduate of the University of California, Santa Barbara and of the University of California, Los Angeles. He is a recipient of the Samuel Goldwyn and Donald Davis Literary Awards

Keep track of what Rob's up to:
www.rmtauthor.com

Ric Wasley

Ric has a 40-year professional career history in advertising, publishing and marketing in Boston, New York and San Francisco. He has degrees in history and psychology and has been trained in debating, public speaking and stage acting. A large part of his career was spent settings as a presenter and featured speaker at seminars and professional meetings. Ric has been a visiting professor at Worcester Polytech Institute. He also teaches a popular course on marketing for authors at prominent venues such as the venerable "Cape Cod Writers Conference". Ric is a published author of a Mystery Series and multiple other novels.